W9-BLF-978

From an etching by Méaulle

VII

SILENCE

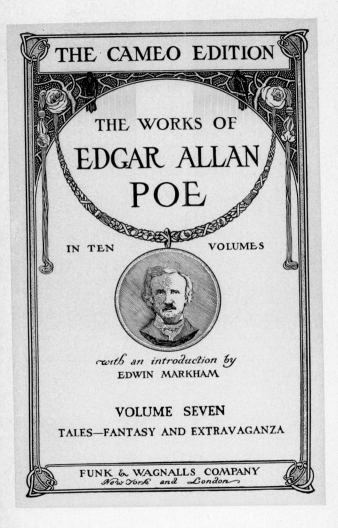

THE CAMEO EDITION

THE WORKS OF
EDGAR ALLAN POE

IN TEN VOLUMES

with an introduction by
EDWIN MARKHAM

VOLUME SEVEN
TALES—FANTASY AND EXTRAVAGANZA

FUNK & WAGNALLS COMPANY
New York and London

COPYRIGHT, 1904

FUNK & WAGNALLS COMPANY

VOLUME VII

TALES—FANTASY AND EXTRAVAGANZA

CONTENTS

THE DOMAIN OF ARNHEIM

[Published in the *Columbian Magazine*, March, 1847.]

The garden like a lady fair was cut,
  That lay as if she slumbered in delight,
And to the open skies her eyes did shut;
  The azure fields of heaven were 'sembled right
  In a large round set with the flowers of light;
The flowers de luce and the round sparks of dew
That hung from their azure leaves did shew
Like twinkling stars that sparkle in the evening blue.
                                        —*Giles Fletcher.*

FROM his cradle to his grave a gale of prosperity bore my friend Ellison along. Nor do I use the word prosperity in its mere worldly sense. I mean it as synonymous with happiness. The person of whom I speak seemed born for the purpose of foreshadowing the doctrines of Turgot, Price, Priestly, and Condorcet—of exemplifying by individual instance what has been deemed the chimera of the perfectionists. In the brief existence of Ellison I fancy that I have seen refuted the dogma, that in man's very nature lies some hidden principle, the antagonist of bliss. An anxious examination of his career has given me to understand that, in general, from the violation of a few simple laws of humanity arises the wretchedness of mankind—that as a

species we have in our possession the as yet unwrought elements of content—and that, even now
in the present darkness and madness of all
thought on the great question of the social condition, it is not impossible that man, the individual,
under certain unusual and highly fortuitous conditions may be happy.

With opinions such as these my young friend,
too, was fully imbued, and thus it is worthy of
observation that the uninterrupted enjoyment
which distinguished his life was, in great measure, the result of preconcert. It is indeed evident that with less of the instinctive philosophy
which, now and then, stands so well in the stead
of experience, Mr. Ellison would have found
himself precipitated, by the very extraordinary
success of his life, into the common vortex of
unhappiness which yawns for those of pre-eminent endowments. But it is by no means my object to pen an essay on happiness. The ideas of
my friend may be summed up in a few words.
He admitted but four elementary principles, or
more strictly, conditions, of bliss. That which he
considered chief was (strange to say!) the simple
and purely physical one of free exercise in the
open air. "The health," he said, "attainable
by other means is scarcely worth the name." He
instanced the ecstasies of the fox-hunter, and
pointed to the tillers of the earth, the only people
who, as a class, can be fairly considered happier
than others. His second condition was the love
of woman. His third, and most difficult of reali-
zation, was the contempt of ambition. His fourth

was an object of unceasing pursuit; and he held
that, other things being equal, the extent of attainable happiness was in proportion to the spirituality of this object.

Ellison was remarkable in the continuous profusion of good gifts lavished upon him by fortune. In personal grace and beauty he exceeded
all men. His intellect was of that order to which
the acquisition of knowledge is less a labor than
an intuition and a necessity. His family was one
of the most illustrious of the empire. His bride
was the loveliest and most devoted of women.
His possessions had been always ample; but on
the attainment of his majority, it was discovered
that one of those extraordinary freaks of fate had
been played in his behalf which startle the whole
social world amid which they occur, and seldom
fail radically to alter the moral constitution of
those who are their objects.

It appears that about a hundred years before
Mr. Ellison's coming of age, there had died, in
a remote province, one Mr. Seabright Ellison.
This gentleman had amassed a princely fortune,
and, having no immediate connections, conceived
the whim of suffering his wealth to accumulate
for a century after his decease. Minutely and
sagaciously directing the various modes of investment, he bequeathed the aggregate amount
to the nearest of blood, bearing the name of Ellison, who should be alive at the end of the hundred years. Many attempts had been made to set
aside this singular bequest; their *ex post facto*
character rendered them abortive; but the atten-

tion of a jealous government was aroused, and a legislative act finally obtained, forbidding all similar accumulations. This act, however, did not prevent young Ellison from entering into possession, on his twenty-first birthday, as the heir of his ancestor Seabright, of a fortune of *four hundred and fifty millions of dollars.**

When it had become known that such was the enormous wealth inherited, there were, of course, many speculations as to the mode of its disposal. The magnitude and the immediate availability of the sum bewildered all who thought on the topic. The possessor of any *appreciable* amount of money might have been imagined to perform any one of a thousand things. With riches merely surpassing those of any citizen, it would have been easy to suppose him engaging to supreme excess in the fashionable extravagances of his time—or busying himself with political intrigue —or aiming at ministerial power—or purchasing increase of nobility—or collecting large museums of *virtu*—or playing the munificent patron of letters, of science, of art—or endowing, and bestowing his name upon extensive institutions of char-

---

* An incident, similar in outline to the one here imagined, occurred, not very long ago, in England. The name of the fortunate heir was Thelluson. I first saw an account of this matter in the " Tour " of Prince Pückler Muskau, who makes the sum inherited *ninety millions of pounds*, and justly observes that " in the contemplation of so vast a sum, and of the services to which it might be applied, there is something even of the sublime." To suit the views of this article I have followed the Prince's statement, although a grossly exaggerated one. The germ, and in fact, the commencement of the present paper was published many years ago—previous to the issue of the first number of Sue's admirable " Juif Errant," which may possibly have been suggested to him by Muskau's account.

ity. But for the inconceivable wealth in the
actual possession of the heir, these objects and
all ordinary objects were felt to afford too limited a field. Recourse was had to figures, and
these but sufficed to confound. It was seen that,
even at three per cent., the annual income of
the inheritance amounted to no less than thirteen
millions and five hundred thousand dollars;
which was one million and one hundred and
twenty-five thousand per month; or thirty-six
thousand nine hundred and eighty-six per day;
or one thousand five hundred and forty-one per
hour; or six and twenty dollars for every minute
that flew. Thus the usual track of supposition
was thoroughly broken up. Men knew not what
to imagine. There were some who even conceived
that Mr. Ellison would divest himself of at least
one-half of his fortune, as of utterly superfluous
opulence—enriching whole troops of his relatives
by division of his superabundance. To the nearest of these he did, in fact, abandon the very
unusual wealth which was his own before the inheritance.

I was not surprised, however, to perceive that
he had long made up his mind on a point which
had occasioned so much discussion to his friends.
Nor was I greatly astonished at the nature of his
decision. In regard to individual charities he
had satisfied his conscience. In the possibility
of any improvement, properly so called, being
effected by man himself in the general condition
of man, he had (I am sorry to confess it) little
faith. Upon the whole, whether happily or un-

happily, he was thrown back, in very great measure, upon self.

In the widest and noblest sense he was a poet. He comprehended, moreover, the true character, the august aims, the supreme majesty and dignity of the poetic sentiment. The fullest, if not the sole proper satisfaction of this sentiment he instinctively felt to lie in the creation of novel forms of beauty. Some peculiarities, either in his early education, or in the nature of his intellect, had tinged with what is termed materialism all his ethical speculations; and it was this bias, perhaps, which led him to believe that the most advantageous at least, if not the sole legitimate field for the poetic exercise, lies in the creation of novel moods of purely *physical* loveliness. Thus it happened he became neither musician nor poet —if we use this latter term in its every-day acceptation. Or it might have been that he neglected to become either, merely in pursuance of his idea that in contempt of ambition is to be found one of the essential principles of happiness on earth. Is it not indeed, possible that, while a high order of genius is necessarily ambitious, the highest is above that which is termed ambition? And may it not thus happen that many far greater than Milton have contentedly remained " mute and inglorious? " I believe that the world has never seen—and that, unless through some series of accidents goading the noblest order of mind into distasteful exertion, the world will never see—that full extent of triumphant exe-

cution, in the richer domains of art, of which
the human nature is absolutely capable.

Ellison became neither musician nor poet; although no man lived more profoundly enamored
of music and poetry. Under other circumstances
than those which invested him, it is not impossible that he would have become a painter. Sculpture, although in its nature rigorously poetical,
was too limited in its extent and consequences,
to have occupied, at any time, much of his attention. And I have now mentioned all the provinces in which the common understanding of the
poetic sentiment has declared it capable of expatiating. But Ellison maintained that the richest, the truest, and most natural, if not altogether the most extensive province, had been un-
accountably neglected. No definition had spoken
of the landscape-gardener as of the poet; yet it
seemed to my friend that the creation of the landscape-garden offered to the proper Muse the most
magnificent of opportunities. Here, indeed, was
the faintest field for the display of imagination
in the endless combining of forms of novel
beauty; the elements to enter into combination
being, by a vast superiority, the most glorious
which the earth could afford. In the multiform
and multicolor of the flowers and the trees, he
recognised the most direct and energetic efforts
of Nature at physical loveliness. And in the
direction or concentration of this effort—or,
more properly, in its adaptation to the eyes
which were to behold it on earth—he perceived
that he should be employing the best means—

laboring to the greatest advantage—in the fulfilment, not only to his own destiny as poet, but of the august purposes for which the Deity had implanted the poetic sentiment in man.

"Its adaptation to the eyes which were to behold it on earth." In his explanation of this phraseology, Mr. Ellison did much toward solving what has always seemed to me an enigma: —I mean the fact (which none but the ignorant dispute) that no such combination of scenery exists in nature as the painter of genius may produce. No such paradises are to be found in reality as have glowed on the canvas of Claude. In the most enchanting of natural landscapes, there will always be found a defect or an excess—many excesses and defects. While the component parts may defy, individually, the highest skill of the artist, the arrangement of these parts will always be susceptible of improvement. In short, no position can be attained on the wide surface of the *natural* earth, from which an artistical eye, looking steadily, will not find matter of offence in what is termed the "composition" of the landscape. And yet how unintelligible is this! In all other matters we are justly instructed to regard nature as supreme. With her details we shrink from competition. Who shall presume to imitate the colors of the tulip, or to improve the proportions of the lily of the valley? The criticism which says, of sculpture or portraiture, that here nature is to be exalted or idealized rather than imitated, is in error. No pictorial or sculptural combinations of points of human loveliness do more than approach the living and breathing beauty. In landscape alone is the principle of the critic true; and, having felt its truth here, it is but the headlong spirit of generalization which has led him to pronounce it true throughout all the domains of art. Having, I say, *felt* its truth here; for the feeling is no affectation or chimera. The mathematics afford no more absolute demonstrations than the sentiments of his art yields the artist. He not only believes, but positively knows, that such and such apparently arbitrary arrangements of matter constitute and alone constitute the true beauty. His reasons, however, have not yet been matured into expression. It remains for a more profound analysis than the world has yet seen, fully to investigate and express them. Nevertheless he is confirmed in his instinctive opinions by the voice of all his brethren. Let a " composition " be defective; let an emendation be wrought in its mere arrangement of form; let this emendation be submitted to every artist in the world; by each will its necessity be admitted. And even far more than this; in remedy of the defective composition, each insulated member of the fraternity would have suggested the identical emendation.

I repeat that in landscape arrangements alone is the physical nature susceptible of exaltation, and that, therefore, her susceptibility of improvement at this one point, was a mystery I had been unable to solve. My own thoughts on the subject had rested in the idea that the primitive intention of nature would have so arranged the earth's

surface as to have fulfilled at all points man's
sense of perfection in the beautiful, the sublime,
or the picturesque; but that this primitive intention had been frustrated by the known geological
disturbances—disturbances of form and color-
grouping, in the correction or allaying of which
lies the soul of art. The force of this idea was
much weakened, however, by the necessity which
it involved of considering the disturbances abnormal and unadapted to any purpose. It was
Ellison who suggested that they were prognostic
of *death*. He thus explained:—Admit the earthly immortality of man to have been the first intention. We have then the primitive arrangement of the earth's surface adapted to his bliss-
ful estate, as not existent but designed. The disturbances were the preparations for his subse-
quently conceived deathful condition.

"Now," said my friend, "what we regard as
exaltation of the landscape may be really such,
as respects only the moral or human *point of
view*. Each alteration of the natural scenery may
possibly effect a blemish in the picture, if we can
suppose this picture viewed at large—in mass—
from some point distant from the earth's surface, although not beyond the limits of its atmosphere. It is easily understood that what might
improve a closely scrutinized detail, may at the
same time injure a general or more distinctly
observed effect. There *may* be a class of beings,
human once, but now invisible to humanity, to
whom, from afar, our disorder may seem order
—our unpicturesqueness picturesque; in a word,

the earth-angels, for whose scrutiny more especially than our own, and for whose death-refined
appreciation of the beautiful, may have been set
in array by God the wide landscape-gardens of
the hemispheres.''

In the course of discussion, my friend quoted
some passages from a writer on landscape-
gardening, who has been supposed to have well
treated his theme:

'' There are properly but two styles of landscape-gardening, the natural and the artificial.
One seeks to recall the original beauty of the
country, by adapting its means to the surrounding scenery; cultivating trees in harmony with
the hills or plains of the neighboring land; detecting and bringing into practice those nice relations of size, proportion and color which, hid
from the common observer, are revealed everywhere to the experienced student of nature. The
result of the natural style of gardening, is seen
rather in the absence of all defects and incongruities—in the prevalence of a healthy harmony
and order—than in the creation of any special
wonders or miracles. The artificial style has as
many varieties as there are different tastes to
gratify. It has a certain general relation to the
various styles of building. There are the stately
avenues and retirements of Versailles; Italian
terraces; and a various mixed old English style,
which bears some relation to the domestic Gothic
or English Elizabethan architecture. Whatever
may be said against the abuses of the artificial
landscape-gardening, a mixture of pure art in

the garden scene adds to it a great beauty. This
is partly pleasing to the eye, by the show of order
and design, and partly moral. A terrace, with
an old moss-covered balustrade, calls up at once
to the eye the fair forms that have passed there
in other days. The slightest exhibition of art
is an evidence of care and human interest.''

" From what I have already observed,'' said
Ellison, " you will understand that I reject the
idea, here expressed, of recalling the original
beauty of the country. The original beauty is
never so great as that which may be introduced.
Of course, every thing depends on the selection
of a spot with capabilities. What is said about
detecting and bringing into practice nice relations of size, proportion, and color, is one of those
mere vaguenesses of speech which serve to veil
inaccuracy of thought. The phrase quoted may
mean any thing, or nothing, and guides in no degree. That the true result of the natural style
of gardening is seen rather in the absence of all
defects and incongruities than in the creation of
any special wonders or miracles, is a proposition
better suited to the grovelling apprehension of
the herd than to the fervid dreams of the man
of genius. The negative merit suggested appertains to that hobbling criticism which, in letters,
would elevate Addison into apotheosis. In truth,
while that virtue which consists in the mere
avoidance of vice appeals directly to the understanding, and can thus be circumscribed in *rule*,
the loftier virtue, which flames in creation, can
be apprehended in its results alone. Rule applies

but to the merits of denial—to the excellencies which refrain. Beyond these, the critical art can but suggest. We may be instructed to build a "Cato," but we are in vain told *how* to conceive a Parthenon or an "Inferno." The thing done, however; the wonder accomplished; and the capacity for apprehension becomes universal. The sophists of the negative school who, through inability to create, have scoffed at creation, are now found the loudest in applause. What, in its chrysalis condition of principle, affronted their demure reason, never fails, in its maturity of accomplishment, to extort admiration from their instinct of beauty.

"The author's observations on the artificial style," continued Ellison, "are less objectionable. A mixture of pure art in a garden scene adds to it a great beauty. This is just; as also is the reference to the sense of human interest. The principle expressed is incontrovertible—but there *may* be something beyond it. There may be an object in keeping with the principle—an object unattainable by the means ordinarily possessed by individuals, yet which, if attained, would lend a charm to the landscape-garden far surpassing that which a sense of merely human interest could bestow. A poet, having very unusual pecuniary resources, might, while retaining the necessary idea of art or culture, or, as our author expresses it, of interest, so imbue his designs at once with extent and novelty of beauty, as to convey the sentiment of spiritual interference. It will be seen that, in bringing

VII. 2

about such result, he secures all the advantages of interest or *design,* while relieving his work of the harshness or technicality of the worldly *art.* In the most rugged of wildernesses—in the most savage of the scenes of pure nature—there is apparent the *art* of a creator; yet this art is apparent to reflection only; in no respect has it the obvious force of a feeling. Now let us suppose this sense of the Almighty design to be *one step depressed*—to be brought into something like harmony or consistency with the sense of human art—to form an intermedium between the two: —let us imagine, for example, a landscape whose combined vastness and definitiveness—whose united beauty, magnificence, and *strangeness,* shall convey the idea of care, or culture, or superintendence, on the part of beings superior, yet akin to humanity—then the sentiment of *interest* is preserved, while the art intervolved is made to assume the air of an intermediate or secondary nature—a nature which is not God, nor an emanation from God, but which still is nature in the sense of the handiwork of the angels that hover between man and God.''

It was in devoting his enormous wealth to the embodiment of a vision such as this—in the free exercise in the open air ensured by the personal superintendence of his plans—in the unceasing object which these plans afforded—in the high spirituality of the object—in the contempt of ambition which it enabled him truly to feel—in the perennial springs with which it gratified, without possibility of satiating, that one master

passion of his soul, the thirst for beauty; above
all, it was in the sympathy of a woman, not un-
womanly, whose loveliness and love enveloped
his existence in the purple atmosphere of Paradise, that Ellison thought to find, *and found,* exemption from the ordinary cares of humanity,
with a far greater amount of positive happiness
than ever glowed in the rapt day-dreams of De
Staël.

I despair of conveying to the reader any distinct conception of the marvels which my friend
did actually accomplish. I wish to describe, but
am disheartened by the difficulty of description,
and hesitate between detail and generality. Perhaps the better course will be to unite the two in
their extremes.

Mr. Ellison's first step regarded, of course, the
choice of a locality; and scarcely had he commenced thinking on this point, when the luxuriant nature of the Pacific Islands arrested his attention. In fact, he had made up his mind for a
voyage to the South Seas, when a night's reflection induced him to abandon the idea. "Were
I misanthropic," he said, "such a *locale* would
suit me. The thoroughness of its insulation and
seclusion, and the difficulty of ingress and egress,
would in such case be the charm of charms; but
as yet I am not Timon. I wish the composure
but not the depression of solitude. There must
remain with me a certain control over the extent
and duration of my repose. There will be frequent hours in which I shall need, too, the sympathy of the poetic in what I have done. Let me

seek, then, a spot not far from a populous city—whose vicinity, also, will best enable me to execute my plans.''

In search of a suitable place so situated, Ellison travelled for several years, and I was permitted to accompany him. A thousand spots with which I was enraptured he rejected without hesitation, for reasons which satisfied me, in the end, that he was right. We came at length to an elevated table-land of wonderful fertility and beauty, affording a panoramic prospect very little less in extent than that of Ætna, and, in Ellison's opinion as well as my own, surpassing the far-famed view from that mountain in all the true elements of the picturesque.

''I am aware,'' said the traveller, as he drew a sigh of deep delight after gazing on this scene, entranced, for nearly an hour, ''I know that here, in my circumstances, nine-tenths of the most fastidious of men would rest content. This panorama is indeed glorious, and I should rejoice in it but for the excess of its glory. The taste of all the architects I have ever known leads them, for the sake of 'prospect,' to put up buildings on hill-tops. The error is obvious. Grandeur in any of its moods, but especially in that of extent, startles, excites—and then fatigues, depresses. For the occasional scene nothing can be better—for the constant view nothing worse. And, in the constant view, the most objectionable phase of grandeur is that of extent; the worst phase of extent, that of distance. It is at war with the sentiment and with the sense of *seclusion*—the sentiment and sense which we seek to humor in 'retiring to the country.' In looking from the summit of a mountain we cannot help feeling *abroad* in the world. The heartsick avoid distant prospects as a pestilence.''

It was not until toward the close of the fourth year of our search that we found a locality with which Ellison professed himself satisfied. It is, of course, needless to say *where* was the locality. The late death of my friend, in causing his domain to be thrown open to certain classes of visitors, has given to *Arnheim* a species of secret and subdued if not solemn celebrity, similar in kind, although infinitely superior in degree, to that which so long distinguished Fonthill.

The usual approach to Arnheim was by the river. The visitor left the city in the early morning. During the forenoon he passed between shores of a tranquil and domestic beauty, on which grazed innumerable sheep, their white fleeces spotting the vivid green of rolling meadows. By degrees the idea of cultivation subsided into that of merely pastoral care. This slowly became merged in a sense of retirement—this again in a consciousness of solitude. As the evening approached, the channel grew more narrow; the banks more and more precipitous; and these latter were clothed in richer, more profuse, and more sombre foliage. The water increased in transparency. The stream took a thousand turns, so that at no moment could its gleaming surface be seen for a greater distance than a furlong. At every instant the vessel seemed imprisoned within an enchanted circle, having insuperable and impenetrable walls of foliage, a roof of ultra-marine satin, and *no* floor—the keel balancing itself with admirable nicety on that of a phantom bark which, by some accident having been turned upside down, floated in constant company with the substantial one, for the purpose of sustaining it. The channel now became a *gorge*—although the term is somewhat inapplicable, and I employ it merely because the language has no word which better represents the most striking—not the most distinctive—feature of the scene. The character of gorge was maintained only in the height and parallelism of the shores; it was lost altogether in their other traits. The walls of the ravine (through which the clear water still tranquilly flowed) arose to an elevation of a hundred and occasionally of a hundred and fifty feet, and inclined so much toward each other as, in a great measure, to shut out the light of day; while the long plume-like moss which depended densely from the intertwining shrubberies overhead, gave the whole chasm an air of funereal gloom. The windings became more frequent and intricate, and seemed often as if returning in upon themselves, so that the voyager had long lost all idea of direction. He was, moreover, enwrapt in an exquisite sense of the strange. The thought of nature still remained, but her character seemed to have undergone modification, there was a weird symmetry, a thrilling uniformity, a wizard propriety in these her works. Not a dead branch—not a withered leaf

—not a stray pebble—not a patch of the brown
earth was anywhere visible. The crystal water
welled up against the clean granite, or the un-
blemished moss, with a sharpness of outline that
delighted while it bewildered the eye.

Having threaded the mazes of this channel for
some hours, the gloom deepening every moment,
a sharp and unexpected turn of the vessel
brought it suddenly, as if dropped from heaven,
into a circular basin of very considerable extent
when compared with the width of the gorge. It
was about two hundred yards in diameter, and
girt it at all points but one—that immediately
fronting the vessel as it entered—by hills equal
in general height to the walls of the chasm, although of a thoroughly different character.
Their sides sloped to the water's edge at an angle
of some forty-five degrees, and they were clothed
from base to summit—not a perceptible point escaping—in a drapery of the most gorgeous flow-
er-blossoms; scarcely a green leaf being visible
among the sea of odorous and fluctuating color.
This basin was of great depth, but so transparent
was the water that the bottom, which seemed to
consist of a thick mass of small round alabaster
pebbles, was distinctly visible by glimpses—that
is to say, whenever the eye could permit itself
not to see, far down in the inverted heaven, the
duplicate blooming of the hills. On these latter
there were no trees, nor even shrubs of any size.
The impressions wrought on the observer were
those of richness, warmth, color, quietude, uniformity, softness, delicacy, daintiness, voluptu-

ousness, and a miraculous extremeness of culture that suggested dreams of a new race of fairies, laborious, tasteful, magnificent, and fastidious; but as the eye traced upward the myriad-tinted slope, from its sharp junction with the water to its vague termination amid the folds of over-hanging cloud, it became, indeed, difficult not to fancy a panoramic cataract of rubies, sapphires, opals, and golden onyxes, rolling silently out of the sky.

The visitor, shooting suddenly into this bay from out the gloom of the ravine, is delighted but astounded by the full orb of the declining sun, which he had supposed to be already far below the horizon, but which now confronts him, and forms the sole termination of an otherwise limit-less vista seen through another chasm-like rift in the hills.

But here the voyager quits the vessel which has borne him so far, and descends into a light canoe of ivory, stained with arabesque devices in vivid scarlet, both within and without. The poop and beak of this boat arise high above the water, with sharp points, so that the general form is that of an irregular crescent. It lies on the sur-face of the bay with the proud grace of a swan. On its ermined floor reposes a single feathery paddle of satin-wood; but no oarsman or atten-dant is to be seen. The guest is bidden to be of good cheer—that the fates will take care of him. The larger vessel disappears, and he is left alone in the canoe, which lies apparently motionless in the middle of the lake. While he considers what course to pursue, however, he becomes aware of a gentle movement in the fairy bark. It slowly swings itself around until its prow points toward the sun. It advances with a gentle but gradually accelerated velocity, while the slight ripples it creates seem to break about the ivory side in divinest melody—seem to offer the only possible explanation of the soothing yet melancholy music for whose unseen origin the bewildered voyager looks around him in vain.

The canoe steadily proceeds, and the rocky gate of the vista is approached, so that its depths can be more distinctly seen. To the right arise a chain of lofty hills rudely and luxuriantly wooded. It is observed, however, that the trait of exquisite *cleanness* where the bank dips into the water, still prevails. There is not one token of the usual river *débris*. To the left the character of the scene is softer and more obviously artificial. Here the bank slopes upward from the stream in a very gentle ascent, forming a broad sward of grass of a texture resembling nothing so much as velvet, and of a brilliancy of green which would bear comparison with the tint of the purest emerald. This *plateau* varies in width from ten to three hundred yards; reaching from the river-bank to a wall, fifty feet high, which extends, in an infinity of curves, but following the general direction of the river, until lost in the distance to the westward. This wall is of one continuous rock, and has been formed by cutting perpendicularly the once rugged precipice of the stream's southern bank; but no trace of the labor

has been suffered to remain. The chiselled stone
has the hue of ages, and is profusely overhung
and overspread with the ivy, the coral honeysuckle, the eglantine, and the clematis. The uniformity of the top and bottom lines of the wall
is fully relieved by occasional trees of gigantic
height, growing singly or in small groups, both
along the *plateau* and in the domain behind the
wall, but in close proximity to it; so that frequent limbs (of the black walnut especially)
reach over and dip their pendent extremities in
the water. Farther back within the domain, the
vision is impeded by an impenetrable screen of
foliage.

These things are observed during the canoe's
gradual approach to what I have called the gate
of the vista. On drawing nearer to this, however, its chasm-like appearance vanishes; a new
outlet from the bay is discovered to the left—in
which direction the wall is also seen to sweep,
still following the general course of the stream.
Down this new opening the eye cannot penetrate
very far; for the stream, accompanied by the
wall, still bends to the left, until both are swallowed up by the leaves.

The boat, nevertheless, glides magically into
the winding channel; and here the shore opposite the wall is found to resemble that opposite
the wall in the straight vista. Lofty hills, rising
occasionally into mountains, and covered with
vegetation in wild luxuriance, still shut in the
scene.

Floating gently onward, but with a velocity

slightly augmented, the voyager, after many
short turns, finds his progress apparently barred
by a gigantic gate or rather door of burnished
gold, elaborately carved and fretted, and reflecting the direct rays of the now fast-sinking sun
with an effulgence that seems to wreathe the
whole surrounding forest in flames. This gate is
inserted in the lofty wall; which here appears
to cross the river at right angles. In a few moments, however, it is seen that the main body of
the water still sweeps in a gentle and extensive
curve to the left, the wall following it as before,
while a stream of considerable volume, diverging
from the principal one, makes its way, with a
slight ripple, under the door, and is thus hidden
from sight. The canoe falls into the lesser channel and approaches the gate. Its ponderous
wings are slowly and musically expanded. The
boat glides between them, and commences a rapid
descent into a vast amphitheatre entirely begirt
with purple mountains, whose bases are laved
by a gleaming river throughout the full extent
of their circuit. Meantime the whole Paradise of
Arnheim bursts upon the view. There is a gush
of entrancing melody; there is an oppressive
sense of strange sweet odor;—there is a dream-
like intermingling to the eye of tall slender Eastern trees—bosky shrubberies—flocks of golden
and crimson birds—lily-fringed lakes—meadows
of violets, tulips, poppies, hyacinths, and tube-
roses—long intertangled lines of silver stream-
lets—and, upspringing confusedly from amid
all, a mass of semi-Gothic, semi-Saracenic archi-

tecture, sustaining itself by miracle in mid-air; glittering in the red sunlight with a hundred oriels, minarets, and pinnacles; and seeming the phantom handiwork, conjointly, of the Sylphs, of the Fairies, of the Genii, and of the Gnomes.*

* See also " The Landscape Garden " in the present volume.
—EDITOR.

LANDOR'S COTTAGE

A PENDANT TO "THE DOMAIN OF ARNHEIM"

[Published in R. W. Griswold's collection of Poe's Works, 1849.]

DURING a pedestrian trip last summer, through one or two of the river counties of New York, I found myself, as the day declined, somewhat embarrassed about the road I was pursuing. The land undulated very remarkably; and my path, for the last hour, had wound about and about so confusedly, in its effort to keep in the valleys, that I no longer knew in what direction lay the sweet village of B———, where I had determined to stop for the night. The sun had scarcely *shone*—strictly speaking—during the day, which, nevertheless, had been unpleasantly warm. A smoky mist, resembling that of the Indian summer, enveloped all things, and of course, added to my uncertainty. Not that I cared much about the matter. If I did not hit upon the village before sunset, or even before dark, it was more than possible that a little Dutch farmhouse, or something of that kind,

would soon make its appearance—although, in
fact, the neighborhood (perhaps on account of
being more picturesque than fertile) was very
sparsely inhabited. At all events, with my knap-
sack for a pillow, and my hound as a sentry, a
bivouac in the open air was just the thing which
would have amused me. I sauntered on, therefore, quite at ease—Ponto taking charge of my
gun—until at length, just as I had begun to consider whether the numerous little glades that led
hither and thither, were intended to be paths at
all, I was conducted by one of them into an un-
questionable carriage track. There could be no
mistaking it. The traces of light wheels were
evident; and although the tall shrubberies and
overgrown undergrowth met overhead, there was
no obstruction whatever below, even to the passage of a Virginian mountain wagon—the most
aspiring vehicle, I take it, of its kind. The road,
however, except in being open through the wood
—if wood be not too weighty a name for such an
assemblage of light trees—and except in the par-
ticulars of evident wheel-tracks—bore no resemblance to any road I had before seen. The tracks
of which I speak were but faintly perceptible—
having been impressed upon the firm, yet pleas-
antly moist surface of—what looked more like
green Genoese velvet than any thing else. It
was grass, clearly—but grass such as we seldom
see out of England—so short, so thick, so even,
and so vivid in color. Not a single impediment
lay in the wheel-route—not even a chip or dead
twig. The stones that once obstructed the way

had been carefully *placed*—not thrown—along the sides of the lane, so as to define its boundaries at bottom with a kind of half-precise, half-negligent, and wholly picturesque definition. Clumps of wild flowers grew everywhere, luxuriantly, in the interspaces.

What to make of all this, of course, I knew not. Here was *art* undoubtedly—*that* did not surprise me—all roads, in the ordinary sense, are works of art; nor can I say that there was much to wonder at in the mere *excess* of art manifested; all that seemed to have been done, might have been done *here*—with such natural "capabilities" (as they have it in the books on Landscape Gardening)—with very little labor and expense. No; it was not the amount but the *character* of the art which caused me to take a seat on one of the blossomy stones and gaze up and down this fairy-like avenue for half an hour or more in bewildered admiration. One thing became more and more evident the longer I gazed: an artist, and one with a most scrupulous eye for form, had superintended all these arrangements. The greatest care had been taken to preserve a due medium between the neat and graceful on the one hand, and the *pittoresque,* in the true sense of the Italian term, on the other. There were few straight, and no long uninterrupted lines. The same effect of curvature or of color appeared twice, usually, but not oftener, at any one point of view. Everywhere was variety in uniformity. It was a piece of "composition," in which the

most fastidiously critical taste could scarcely
have suggested an emendation.

I had turned to the right as I entered this
road, and now, arising, I continued in the same
direction. The path was so serpentine, that at
no moment could I trace its course for more than
two or three paces in advance. Its character did
not undergo any material change.

Presently the murmur of water fell gently
upon my ear—and in a few moments afterward,
as I turned with the road somewhat more
abruptly than hitherto, I became aware that a
building of some kind lay at the foot of a gentle
declivity just before me. I could see nothing
distinctly on account of the mist which occupied
all the little valley below. A gentle breeze, however, now arose, as the sun was about descending; and while I remained standing on the brow
of the slope, the fog gradually became dissipated
into wreaths, and so floated over the scene.

As it came fully into view—thus *gradually* as
I describe it—piece by piece, here a tree, there a
glimpse of water, and here again the summit of
a chimney, I could scarcely help fancying that
the whole was one of the ingenious illusions
sometimes exhibited under the name of "vanish-
ing pictures."

By the time, however, that the fog had thoroughly disappeared, the sun had made its way
down behind the gentle hills, and thence, as if
with a slight *chassez* to the south, had come again
fully into sight, glaring with a purplish lustre
through a chasm that entered the valley from the

west. Suddenly, therefore—and as if by the hand of magic—this whole valley and every thing in it became brilliantly visible.

The first *coup d' œil*, as the sun slid into the position described, impressed me very much as I have been impressed, when a boy, by the concluding scene of some well-arranged theatrical spectacle or melodrama. Not even the monstrosity of color was wanting; for the sunlight came out through the chasm, tinted all orange and purple; while the vivid green of the grass in the valley was reflected more or less upon all objects from the curtain of vapor that still hung overhead, as if loth to take its total departure from a scene so enchantingly beautiful.

The little vale into which I thus peered down from under the fog-canopy could not have been more than four hundred yards long; while in breadth it varied from fifty to one hundred and fifty or perhaps two hundred. It was most narrow at its northern extremity, opening out as it tended southwardly, but with no very precise regularity. The widest portion was within eighty yards of the southern extreme. The slopes which encompassed the vale could not fairly be called hills, unless at their northern face. Here a precipitous ledge of granite arose to a height of some ninety feet; and, as I have mentioned, the valley at this point was not more than fifty feet wide; but as the visitor proceeded southwardly from this cliff, he found on his right hand and on his left, declivities at once less high, less precipitous, and less rocky. All in a

VII. 3

word, sloped and softened to the south; and yet
the whole vale was engirdled by eminences, more
or less high, except at two points. One of these
I have already spoken of. It lay considerably
to the north of west, and was where the setting
sun made its way, as I have before described,
into the amphitheatre, through a clean cut natural cleft in the granite embankment; this fis-
sure might have been ten yards wide at its widest point, so far as the eye could trace it. It
seemed to lead up, up like a natural causeway,
into the recesses of unexplored mountains and
forests. The other opening was directly at the
southern end of the vale. Here, generally, the
slopes were nothing more than gentle inclinations, extending from east to west about one hundred and fifty yards. In the middle of this extent was a depression, level with the ordinary
floor of the valley. As regards vegetation, as
well as in respect to every thing else, the scene
softened and sloped to the south. To the north
—on the craggy precipice—a few paces from the
verge—upsprang the magnificent trunks of numerous hickories, black walnuts, and chestnuts,
interspersed with occasional oak; and the strong
lateral branches thrown out by the walnuts especially, spread far over the edge of the cliff.
Proceeding southwardly, the explorer saw, at first
the same class of trees, but less and less lofty and
Salvatorish in character; then he saw the gen-
tler elm, succeeded by the sassafras and locust—
these again by the softer linden, red-bud, catalpa,
and maple—these yet again by still more grace-

ful and more modest varieties. The whole face
of the southern declivity was covered with wild
shrubbery alone—an occasional silver willow or
white poplar excepted. In the bottom of the
valley itself—(for it must be borne in mind that
the vegetation hitherto mentioned grew only on
the cliffs or hillsides)—were to be seen three insulated trees. One was an elm of fine size and
exquisite form: it stood guard over the southern
gate of the vale. Another was a hickory, much
larger than the elm, and altogether a much finer
tree, although both were exceedingly beautiful:
it seemed to have taken charge of the north-
western entrance, springing from a group of
rocks in the very jaws of the ravine, and throwing its graceful body, at an angle of nearly forty-
five degrees, far out into the sunshine of the
amphitheatre. About thirty yards east of this
tree stood, however, the pride of the valley, and
beyond all question the most magnificent tree I
have ever seen, unless, perhaps, among the
cypresses of the Itchiatuckanee. It was a triple-
stemmed tulip-tree—the *Liriodendron Tulipi-*
ferum—one of the natural order of magnolias.
Its three trunks separated from the parent at
about three feet from the soil, and diverging very
slightly and gradually, were not more than four
feet apart at the point where the largest stem
shot out into foliage: this was at an elevation of
about eighty feet. The whole height of the principal division was one hundred and twenty feet.
Nothing can surpass in beauty the form, or the
glossy, vivid green of the leaves of the tulip-tree.

In the present instance they were fully eight inches wide; but their glory was altogether eclipsed by the gorgeous splendor of the profuse blossoms. Conceive, closely congregated, a million of the largest and most resplendent tulips! Only thus can the reader get any idea of the picture I would convey. And then the stately grace of the clean, delicately granulated columnar stems, the largest four feet in diameter, at twenty from the ground. The innumerable blossoms, mingling with those of other trees scarcely less beautiful, although infinitely less majestic, filled the valley with more than Arabian perfumes.

The general floor of the amphitheatre was *grass* of the same character as that I had found in the road; if any thing, more deliciously soft, thick, velvety, and miraculously green. It was hard to conceive how all this beauty had been attained.

I have spoken of two openings into the vale. From the one to the north-west issued a rivulet, which came, gently murmuring and slightly foaming, down the ravine, until it dashed against the group of rocks out of which sprang the insulated hickory. Here, after encircling the tree, it passed on a little to the north of east, leaving the tulip tree some twenty feet to the south, and making no decided alteration in its course until it came near the midway between the eastern and western boundaries of the valley. At this point, after a series of sweeps, it turned off at right angles and pursued a generally

southern direction—meandering as it went—
until it became lost in a small lake of irregular
figure (although roughly oval), that lay gleaming near the lower extremity of the vale. This
lakelet was, perhaps, a hundred yards in diameter at its widest part. No crystal could be
clearer than its waters. Its bottom, which could
be distinctly seen, consisted altogether of pebbles
brilliantly white. Its banks, of the emerald
grass already described, *rounded*, rather than
sloped, off into the clear heaven below; and *so*
clear was this heaven, so perfectly, at times, did
it reflect all objects above it, that where the true
bank ended and where the mimic one commenced,
it was a point of no little difficulty to determine.
The trout, and some other varieties of fish, with
which this pond seemed to be almost inconveni-
ently crowded, had all the appearance of veri-
table flying-fish. It was almost impossible to believe that they were not absolutely suspended in
the air. A light birch canoe that lay placidly on
the water, was reflected in its minutest fibres
with a fidelity unsurpassed by the most exquisitely polished mirror. A small island, fairly
laughing with flowers in full bloom, and affording little more space than just enough for a picturesque little building, seemingly a fowl-house
—arose from the lake not far from its northern
shore—to which it was connected by means of
an inconceivably light-looking and yet very
primitive bridge. It was formed of a single,
broad and thick plank of the tulip wood. This
was forty feet long, and spanned the interval

between shore and shore with a slight but very perceptible arch, preventing all oscillation. From the southern extreme of the lake issued a continuation of the rivulet, which, after meandering for, perhaps, thirty yards, finally passed through the "depression" (already described) in the middle of the southern declivity, and tumbling down a sheer precipice of a hundred feet, made its devious and unnoticed way to the Hudson.

The lake was deep—at some points thirty feet —but the rivulet seldom exceeded three, while its greatest width was about eight. Its bottom and banks were as those of the pond—if a defect could have been attributed, in point of picturesqueness, it was that of excessive *neatness*.

The expanse of the green turf was relieved, here and there, by an occasional showy shrub, such as the hydrangea, or the common snow-ball, or the aromatic syringa; or, more frequently, by a clump of geraniums blossoming gorgeously in great varieties. These latter grew in pots which were carefully buried in the soil, so as to give the plants the appearance of being indigenous. Besides all this, the lawn's velvet was exquisitely spotted with sheep—a considerable flock of which roamed about the vale, in company with three tamed deer, and a vast number of brilliantly plumed ducks. A very large mastiff seemed to be in vigilant attendance upon these animals, each and all.

Along the eastern and western cliffs—where, toward the upper portion of the amphitheatre,

the boundaries were more or less precipitous—
grew ivy in great profusion—so that only here
and there could even a glimpse of the naked
rock be obtained. The northern precipice, in
like manner, was almost entirely clothed by
grape-vines of rare luxuriance; some springing
from the soil at the base of the cliff, and others
from ledges on its face.

The slight elevation which formed the lower
boundary of this little domain, was crowned by a
neat stone wall, of sufficient height to prevent
the escape of the deer. Nothing of the fence
kind was observable elsewhere, for nowhere else
was an artificial enclosure needed:—any stray
sheep, for example, which should attempt to
make its way out of the vale by means of the
ravine, would find its progress arrested, after a
few yards' advance, by the precipitous ledge of
rock over which tumbled the cascade that had
arrested my attention as I first drew near the
domain. In short, the only ingress or egress
was through a gate occupying a rocky pass in the
road, a few paces below the point at which I
stopped to reconnoitre the scene.

I have described the brook as meandering very
irregularly through the whole of its course. Its
two *general* directions, as I have said, were first
from west to east, and then from north to south.
At the *turn*, the stream, sweeping backward,
made an almost circular *loop*, so as to form a
peninsula which was *very* nearly an island, and
which included about the sixteenth of an acre.
On this peninsula stood a dwelling-house—and

when I say that this house, like the infernal terrace seen at Vathek, *"était d'une architecture inconnue dans les annales de la terre,"* I mean, merely, that its *tout ensemble* struck me with the keenest sense of combined novelty and propriety —in a word, of *poetry*—(for, than in the words just employed, I could scarcely give, of poetry in the abstract, a more rigorous definition)—and I do *not* mean that the merely *outré* was perceptible in any respect.

In fact nothing could well be more simple— more utterly unpretending than this cottage. Its marvellous *effect* lay altogether in its artistic arrangement *as a picture.* I could have fancied, while I looked at it, that some eminent landscapepainter had built it with his brush.

The point of view from which I first saw the valley, was not *altogether,* although it was nearly, the best point from which to survey the house. I will therefore describe it as I afterwards saw it—from a position on the stone wall at the southern extreme of the amphitheatre.

The main building was about twenty-four feet long and sixteen broad—certainly not more. Its total height, from the ground to the apex of the roof, could not have exceeded eighteen feet. To the west end of this structure was attached one about a third smaller in all its proportions:—the line of its front standing back about two yards from that of the larger house; and the line of its roof, of course, being considerably depressed below that of the roof adjoining. At right angles to these buildings, and from the rear of the main one—not exactly in the middle—extended a third compartment, very small—being, in general, one third lesss than the western wing. The roofs of the two larger were very steep—sweeping down from the ridge-beam with a long concave curve, and extending at least four feet beyond the walls in front, so as to form the roofs of two piazzas. These latter roofs, of course, needed no support; but as they had the *air* of needing it, slight and perfectly plain pillars were inserted at the corners alone. The roof of the northern wing was merely an extension of a portion of the main roof. Between the chief building and western wing arose a very tall and rather slender square chimney of hard Dutch bricks, alternately black and red:—a slight cornice of projecting bricks at the top. Over the gables the roofs also projected very much:—in the main building about four feet to the east and two to the west. The principal door was not exactly in the main division, being a little to the east—while the two windows were to the west. These latter did not extend to the floor, but were much longer and narrower than usual—they had single shutters like doors— the panes were of lozenge form, but quite large. The door itself had its upper half of glass, also in lozenge panes—a movable shutter secured it at night. The door to the west wing was in its gable, and quite simple—a single window looked out to the south. There was no external door to the north wing, and it also had only one window to the east.

The blank wall of the eastern gable was relieved by stairs (with a balustrade) running diagonally across it—the ascent being from the south. Under cover of the widely projecting cave these steps gave access to a door leading into the garret, or rather loft—for it was lighted only by a single window to the north, and seemed to have been intended as a store room.

The piazzas of the main building and western wing had no floors, as is usual; but at the doors and at each window, large, flat, irregular slabs of granite lay imbedded in the delicious turf, affording comfortable footing in all weather. Excellent paths of the same material—not *nicely* adapted, but with the velvety sod filling frequent intervals between the stones, led hither and thither from the house, to a crystal spring about five paces off, to the road, or to one or two outhouses that lay to the north, beyond the brook, and were thoroughly concealed by a few locusts and catalpas.

Not more than six steps from the main door of the cottage stood the dead trunk of a fantastic pear-tree, so clothed from head to foot in the gorgeous begonia blossoms that one required no little scrutiny to determine what manner of sweet thing it could be. From various arms of this tree hung cages of different kinds. In one, a large wicker cylinder with a ring at top, revelled a mocking bird; in another an oriole; in a third the impudent bobolink—while three or four more delicate prisons were loudly vocal with canaries.

The pillars of the piazza were enwreathed in jasmine and sweet honeysuckle; while from the angle formed by the main structure and its west wing, in front, sprang a grape-vine of unexampled luxuriance. Scorning all restraint, it had clambered first to the lower roof—then to the higher; and along the ridge of this latter it continued to writhe on, throwing out tendrils to the right and left, until at length it fairly attained the east gable, and fell trailing over the stairs.

The whole house, with its wings, was constructed of the old-fashioned Dutch shingles—broad, and with unrounded corners. It is a peculiarity of this material to give houses built of it the appearance of being wider at bottom than at top—after the manner of Egyptian architecture; and in the present instance, this exceedingly picturesque effect was aided by numerous pots of gorgeous flowers that almost encompassed the base of the buildings.

The shingles were painted a dull gray; and the happiness with which this neutral tint melted into the vivid green of the tulip tree leaves that partially overshadowed the cottage, can readily be conceived by an artist.

From the position near the stone wall, as described, the buildings were seen at great advantage—for the south-eastern angle was thrown forward—so that the eye took in at once the whole of the two fronts, with the picturesque eastern gable, and at the same time obtained just a sufficient glimpse of the northern wing, with parts of a pretty roof to the spring-house, and nearly half of a light bridge that spanned the brook in the near vicinity of the main buildings.

I did not remain very long on the brow of the hill, although long enough to make a thorough survey of the scene at my feet. It was clear that I had wandered from the road to the village, and I had thus good travellers' excuse to open the gate before me, and inquire my way, at all events; so, without more ado, I proceeded.

The road, after passing the gate, seemed to lie upon a natural ledge, sloping gradually down along the face of the north-eastern cliffs. It led me on to the foot of the northern precipice, and thence over the bridge, round by the eastern gable to the front door. In this progress, I took notice that no sight of the out-houses could be obtained.

As I turned the corner of the gable, the mastiff bounded towards me in stern silence, but with the eye and the whole air of a tiger. I held him out my hand, however, in token of amity—and I never yet knew the dog who was proof against such an appeal to his courtesy. He not only shut his mouth and wagged his tail, but absolutely offered me his paw—afterward extending his civilities to Ponto.

As no bell was discernible, I rapped with my stick against the door, which stood half open. Instantly a figure advanced to the threshold—that of a young woman about twenty-eight years of age—slender, or rather slight, and somewhat above the medium height. As she approached, with a certain *modest decision* of step altogether indescribable, I said to myself, "Surely here I have found the perfection of natural, in contra-

distinction from artificial *grace.*'' The second
impression which she made on me, but by far the
more vivid of the two, was that of *enthusiasm.*
So intense an expression of *romance,* perhaps I
should call it, or of unworldiness, as that which
gleamed from her deep-set eyes, had never so
sunk into my heart of hearts before. I know not
how it is, but this peculiar expression of the eye,
wreathing itself occasionally into the lips, is the
most powerful, if not absolutely the *sole* spell,
which rivets my interest in woman. '' *Romance,*''
provided my readers fully comprehend what I
would here imply by the word—'' romance '' and
'' womanliness '' seem to me convertible terms:
and, after all, what man truly *loves* in woman, is
simply, her *womanhood.* The eyes of Annie (I
heard some one from the interior call her '' Annie, darling! '') were '' spiritual gray;'' her
hair, a light chestnut: this is all I had time to
observe of her.

At her most courteous of invitations, I entered
—passing first into a tolerably wide vestibule.
Having come mainly to *observe,* I took notice
that to my right as I stepped in, was a window,
such as those in front of the house; to the left,
a door leading into the principal room; while,
opposite me, an *open* door enabled me to see a
small apartment, just the size of the vestibule,
arranged as a study, and having a large *bow*
window looking out to the north.

Passing into the parlor, I found myself with
Mr. Landor—for this, I afterwards found, was
his name. He was civil, even cordial in his man-

ner; but just then, I was more intent on observing the arrangements of the dwelling which had so much interested me, than the personal appearance of the tenant.

The north wing, I now saw, was a bedchamber; its door opened into the parlor. West of this door was a single window, looking toward the brook. At the west end of the parlor, were a fire-place, and a door leading into the west wing—probably a kitchen.

Nothing could be more rigorously simple than the furniture of the parlor. On the floor was an ingrain carpet, of excellent texture—a white ground, spotted with small circular green figures. At the windows were curtains of snowy white jaconet muslin: they were tolerably full, and hung *decisively*, perhaps rather formally in sharp, parallel plaits to the floor—*just* to the floor. The walls were prepared with a French paper of great delicacy, a silver ground, with a faint green cord running zig-zag throughout. Its expanse was relieved merely by three of Julien's exquisite lithographs *à trois crayons,* fastened to the wall without frames. One of these drawings was a scene of Oriental luxury, or rather voluptuousness; another was a '' carnival piece,'' spirited beyond compare; the third was a Greek female head—a face so divinely beautiful, and yet of an expression so provokingly indeterminate, never before arrested my attention.

The more substantial furniture consisted of a round table, a few chairs (including a large rocking-chair), and a sofa, or rather '' settee ''; its material was plain maple painted a creamy white, slightly interstriped with green—the seat of cane. The chairs and table were " to match "; but the *forms* of all had evidently been designed by the same brain which planned " the grounds "; it is impossible to conceive any thing more graceful.

On the table were a few books; a large, square, crystal bottle of some novel perfume; a plain, ground glass *astral* (not solar) lamp, with an Italian shade; and a large vase of resplendently-blooming flowers. Flowers indeed of gorgeous colors and delicate odor formed the sole mere *decoration* of the apartment. The fire-place was nearly filled with a vase of brilliant geranium. On a triangular shelf in each angle of the room stood also a similar vase, varied only as to its lovely contents. One or two smaller *bouquets* adorned the mantel; and late violets clustered about the open windows.

It is not the purpose of this work to do more than give, in detail, a picture of Mr. Landor's residence—*as I found it.*

THE LANDSCAPE GARDEN *

[Published in *Snowden's Lady's Companion*, October 1842.]

> The garden like a lady fair was cut,
>   That lay as if she slumbered in delight,
> And to the open skies her eyes did shut;
>   The azure fields of heaven were 'sembled right
>   In a large round set with the flow'rs of light;
> The flowers de luce and the round sparks of dew
> That hung upon their azure leaves did shew
> Like twinkling stars that sparkle in the evening blue.
>
> —*Giles Fletcher.*

No more remarkable man ever lived than my friend, the young Ellison. He was remarkable in the entire and continuous profusion of good gifts ever lavished upon him by fortune. From his cradle to his grave, a gale of the blandest prosperity bore him along. Nor do I use the word Prosperity in its mere worldly or external sense. I mean it as synonymous with happiness. The person of whom I speak seemed born for the purpose of foreshadowing the wild doctrines of Turgot, Price, Priestley, and Condorcet—of exemplifying, by individual instance, what has been the mere chimera of the perfectionists. In the brief existence of Ellison, I fancy that I have seen re-

---

* See also "The Domain of Arnheim" in the present volume.—EDITOR.

futed the dogma—that in man's physical and spiritual nature lies some hidden principle, the antagonist of Bliss. An intimate and anxious examination of his career has taught me to understand that, in general, from the violation of a few simple laws of Humanity, arises the Wretchedness of mankind; that, as a species, we have in our possession the as yet unwrought elements of Content; and that, even now, in the present blindness and darkness of all idea on the great question of the Social Condition, it is not impossible that Man, the individual, under certain unusual and highly fortuitous conditions, may be happy.

With opinions such as these was my young friend fully imbued; and thus is it especially worthy of observation that the uninterrupted enjoyment which distinguished his life was in great part the result of preconcert. It is, indeed, evident, that with less of the instinctive philosophy which, now and then, stands so well in the stead of experience, Mr. Ellison would have found himself precipitated, by the very extraordinary successes of his life, into the common vortex of Unhappiness which yawns for those of pre-eminent endowments. But it is by no means my present object to pen an essay on Happiness. The ideas of my friend may be summed up in a few words. He admitted but four unvarying laws, or rather elementary principles, of Bliss. That which he considered chief, was (strange to say!) the simple and purely physical one of free exercise in the open air. "The health," he said,

VII. 4

" attainable by other means than this is scarcely worth the name." He pointed to the tillers of the earth—the only people who, as a class, are proverbially more happy than others—and then he instanced the high ecstasies of the fox-hunter. His second principle was the love of woman. His third was the contempt of ambition. His fourth was an object of unceasing pursuit; and he held that, other things being equal, the extent of happiness was proportioned to the spirituality of this object.

I have said that Ellison was remarkable in the continuous profusion of good gifts lavished upon him by Fortune. In personal grace and beauty he exceeded all men. His intellect was of that order to which the attainment of knowledge is less a labor than a necessity and an intuition. His family was one of the most illustrious of the empire. His bride was the loveliest and most devoted of women. His possessions had been always ample, but, upon the attainment of his one and twentieth year, it was discovered that one of those extraordinary freaks of Fate had been played in his behalf, which startle the whole social world amid which they occur, and seldom fail radically to alter the entire moral constitution of those who are their objects. It appears that about one hundred years prior to Mr. Ellison's attainment of his majority, there had died, in a remote province, one Mr. Seabright Ellison. This gentleman had amassed a princely fortune, and, having no very immediate connections, conceived the whim of suffering his wealth to accu-

mulate for a century after his decease. Minutely
and sagaciously directing the various modes of
investment, he bequeathed the aggregate amount
to the nearest of blood, bearing the name Ellison,
who should be alive at the end of the hundred
years.   Many futile attempts had been made to
set aside this singular bequest; their *ex post facto*
character rendered them abortive; but the attention of a jealous government was aroused, and
a decree finally obtained, forbidding all similar
accumulations.   This act did not prevent young
Ellison, upon his twenty-first birthday, from entering into possession, as the heir of his ancestor
Seabright, of a fortune of *four hundred and fifty
millions of dollars.**

When it had become definitely known that
such was the enormous wealth inherited, there
were, of course, many speculations as to the mode
of its disposal.   The gigantic magnitude and the
immediately available nature of the sum, dazzled
and bewildered all who thought upon the topic.
The possessor of any *appreciable* amount of
money might have been imagined to perform any
one of a thousand things.   With riches merely
surpassing those of any citizen, it would have
been easy to suppose him engaging to supreme

* An incident similar in outline to the one here imagined
occurred, not very long ago, in England.   The name of the
fortunate heir (who still lives) is Thelluson.   I first saw an
account of this matter in the " Tour " of Prince Pückler Muskau.   He makes the sum received ninety millions of pounds,
and observes, with much force, that " in the contemplation of
so vast a sum, and to the services to which it might be applied, there is something even of the sublime."   To suit the
views of this article, I have followed the Prince's statement
—a grossly exaggerated one, no doubt.

excess in the fashionable extravagances of his
time; or busying himself with political intrigues;
or aiming at ministerial power; or purchasing
increase of nobility; or devising gorgeous archi-
tectural piles; or collecting large specimens of
Virtu; or playing the munificent patron of Letters and Art; or endowing and bestowing his
name upon extensive institutions of charity. But,
for the inconceivable wealth in the actual possession of the young heir, these objects and all ordinary objects were felt to be inadequate.   Recourse was had to figures; and figures but sufficed
to confound.   It was seen, that even at three per
cent., the annual income of the inheritance
amounted to no less than thirteen millions and
five hundred thousand dollars; which was one
million and one hundred and twenty-five thousand per month; or thirty-six thousand, nine
hundred and eighty-six per day; or one thousand
five hundred and forty-one per hour; or six and
twenty dollars for every minute that flew. Thus,
the usual track of supposition was thoroughly
broken up.   Men knew not what to imagine.
There were some who even conceived that Mr.
Ellison would divest himself forthwith of at
least two thirds of his fortune as of utterly superfluous opulence; enriching whole troops of his
relatives by division of his superabundance.

I was not surprised, however, to perceive that
he had long made up his mind upon a topic which
had occasioned so much of discussion to his
friends.   Nor was I greatly astonished at the
nature of his decision.   In the widest and noblest

sense, he was a poet. He comprehended, moreover, the true character, the august aims, the supreme majesty and dignity of the poetic sentiment. The proper gratification of the sentiment he instinctively felt to lie in the *creation of novel forms of Beauty.* Some peculiarities, either in his early education, or in the nature of his intellect, had tinged with what is termed materialism the whole cast of his ethical speculations; and it was this bias, perhaps, which imperceptibly led him to perceive that the most advantageous, if not the sole legitimate field for the exercise of the poetic sentiment, was to be found in the creation of novel moods of purely *physical* loveliness. Thus it happened that he became neither musician nor poet, if we use this latter term in its every-day acceptation. Or it might have been that he became neither the one nor the other, in pursuance of an idea of his which I have already mentioned—the idea, that in the contempt of ambition lay one of the essential principles of happiness on earth. Is it not, indeed, possible that while a *high* order of genius is necessarily ambitious, the *highest* is invariably *above* that which is termed ambition? And may it not thus happen that many far greater than Milton, have contentedly remained "mute and inglorious?" I believe that the world has never yet seen, and that, unless through some series of accidents goading the noblest order of mind into distasteful exertion, the world will *never* behold that full extent of triumphant execution, in the richer productions of Art, of which the human nature is absolutely capable.

Mr. Ellison became neither musician nor poet; although no man lived more profoundly enamored both of Music and the Muse. Under other circumstances than those which invested him, it is not impossible that he would have become a painter. The field of sculpture, although in its nature rigidly poetical, was too limited in its extent and in its consequences to have occupied, at any time, much of his attention. And I have now mentioned *all* the provinces in which even the most liberal understanding of the poetic sentiment has declared this sentiment capable of expatiating. I mean the most liberal public or recognized conception of the idea involved in the phrase "poetic sentiment." But Mr. Ellison imagined that the richest, and altogether the most natural and most suitable province, had been blindly neglected. No definition had spoken of the *Landscape-Gardener,* or of the poet; yet my friend could not fail to perceive that the creation of the Landscape-Garden offered to the true muse the most magnificent of opportunities. Here was, indeed, the fairest field for the display of invention, or imagination, in the endless combining of forms of novel Beauty; the elements which should enter into combination being, at all times, and by a vast superiority, the most glorious which the earth could afford. In the multiform of the tree, and in the multicolor of the flower, he recognized the most direct and the most energetic efforts of Nature at physical loveliness. And in the direction or concentration of this effort, or, still more properly, in its adaptation to the eyes which were to behold it upon earth, he perceived that he should be employing the best means—laboring to the greatest advantage—in the fulfilment of his destiny as Poet.

"Its adaptation to the eyes which were to behold it upon earth." In his explanation of this phraseology, Mr. Ellison did much toward solving what has always seemed to me an enigma. I mean the fact (which none but the ignorant dispute), that no such combinations of scenery exist in Nature as the painter of genius has in his power to produce. No such Paradises are to be found in reality as have glowed upon the canvas of Claude. In the most enchanting of natural landscapes, there will always be found a defect or an excess—many excesses and defects. While the component parts may exceed, individually, the highest skill of the artist, the arrangement of the parts will always be susceptible of improvement. In short, no position can be attained, from which an artistical eye, looking steadily, will not find matter of offence, in what is technically termed the *composition* of a natural landscape. And yet how unintelligible is this. In all other matters we are justly instructed to regard Nature as supreme. With her details we shrink from competition. Who shall presume to imitate the colors of the tulip, or to improve the proportions of the lily of the valley? The criticism which says, of sculpture or of portraiture, that "Nature is to be exalted rather than imitated," is in error. No pictorial or sculptural combinations of *points* of human loveliness do more than approach the living and breathing human beauty as it gladdens our daily path. Byron, who often erred, erred not in saying:

> I've seen more living beauty, ripe and real,
> Than all the nonsense of their stone ideal.

In landscape alone is the principle of the critic true; and, having felt its truth here, it is but the headlong spirit of generalization which has induced him to pronounce it true throughout *all* the domains of Art. Having, I say, *felt* its truth here. For the feeling is no affectation or chimera. The mathematics afford no more absolute demonstrations, than the *sentiment* of his Art yields to the artist. He not only believes, but positively *knows,* that such and such apparently arbitrary arrangements of matter, or form, constitute, and alone constitute, the true Beauty. Yet his reasons have not yet been matured into expansion. It remains for a more profound analysis than the world has yet seen, fully to investigate and express them. Nevertheless is he confirmed in his instinctive opinions by the concurrence of all his compeers. Let a composition be defective; let an emendation be wrought in its mere arrangement of form; let this emendation be submitted to every artist in the world; by each will its necessity be admitted. And even far more than this; in remedy of the defective composition, each insulated member of the fraternity will suggest the identical emendation.

I repeat that in landscape arrangements, or collocations alone, is the *physical* Nature susceptible of "exaltation," and that, therefore, her susceptibility of improvement at this one point, was a mystery which, hitherto, I had been unable to solve. It was Mr. Ellison who first suggested the idea that what we regarded as improvement or exaltation of the natural beauty, was really such, as respected only the mortal or human *point of view;* that each alteration or disturbance of the primitive scenery might possibly effect a blemish in the picture, if we could suppose this picture viewed *at large* from some remote point in the heavens. "It is easily understood," says Mr. Ellison, "that what might improve a closely scrutinized detail might at the same time, injure a general and more distantly observed effect." He spoke upon this topic with warmth: regarding not so much its immediate or obvious importance (which is little), as the character of the conclusions to which it might lead, or of the collateral propositions which it might serve to corroborate or sustain. There *might be* a class of beings, human once, but now to humanity invisible, for whose scrutiny, and for whose refined appreciation of the beautiful, more especially than for our own, had been set in order by God the great landscape-garden of *the whole earth.*

In the course of our discussion, my young friend took occasion to quote some passages from a writer who has been supposed to have well treated this theme.

"There are, properly," he writes, "but two styles of landscape-gardening, the natural and the artificial. One seeks to recall the original beauty of the country, by adapting its means to the surrounding scenery; cultivating trees in harmony with the hills or plains of the neighboring land; detecting and bringing into practice those nice relations of size, proportion, and color which, hid from the common observer, are revealed everywhere to the experienced student of nature. The result of the natural style of gardening is seen rather in the absence of all defects and incongruities, in the prevalence of a beautiful harmony and order, than in the creation of any special wonders or miracles. The artificial style has as many varieties as there are different tastes to gratify. It has a certain general relation to the various styles of building. There are the stately avenues and retirements of Versailles; Italian terraces; and a various mixed old English style, which bears some relation to the domestic Gothic or English Elizabethan architecture. Whatever may be said against the abuses of the artificial landscape-gardening, a mixture of pure art in a garden scene adds to it a great beauty. This is partly pleasing to the eye, by the show of order and design, and partly moral. A terrace, with an old moss-covered balustrade, calls up at once to the eye the fair forms that have passed there in other days. The slightest exhibition of art is an evidence of care and human interest.''

''From what I have already observed,'' said Mr. Ellison, ''you will understand that I reject the idea, here expressed, of 'recalling the original beauty of the country.' The original beauty is never so great as that which may be introduced. Of course much depends upon the selection of a spot with *capabilities*. What is said in respect to the 'detecting and bringing into practice those nice relations of size, proportion, and color,' is a mere vagueness of speech, which may mean much, or little, or nothing, and which guides in no degree. That the true 'result of the natural style of gardening is seen rather in the absence of all defects and incongruities, than in the creation of any special wonders or miracles,' is a proposition better suited to the grovelling apprehension of the herd than to the fervid dreams of the man of genius. The merit suggested, is, at best, negative, and appertains to that hobbling criticism which, in letters, would elevate Addison into apotheosis. In truth, while that merit which consists in the mere avoiding demerit, appeals directly to the understanding, and can thus be foreshadowed in *Rule*, the loftier merit, which breathes and flames in invention or creation, can be apprehended solely in its results. Rule applies but to the excellence of avoidance—to the virtues which deny or refrain. Beyond these the critical art can but suggest. We may be instructed to build an Odyssey, but it is in vain that we are told *how* to conceive a 'Tempest,' an 'Inferno,' a 'Prometheus Bound,' a 'Nightingale' such as that of Keats, or the 'Sensitive Plant' of Shelley. But, the thing done, the wonder accomplished, and the capacity for apprehension becomes universal. The sophists of the *negative* school, who, through inability to create, have scoffed at creation, are now found the loudest in applause. What, in its chrysalis condition of principle, affronted their demure reason, never fails, in its maturity of accomplishment, to extort admiration from their instinct of the beautiful or of the sublime.

"Our author's observations on the artificial style of gardening," continued Mr. Ellison, "are less objectionable. 'A mixture of pure art in a garden scene adds to it a great beauty.' This is just, and the reference to the sense of human interest is equally so. I repeat that the principle here expressed is incontrovertible; but there *may be* something even beyond it. There may be an object in full keeping with the principle suggested—an object unattainable by the means ordinarily in possession of mankind, yet which, if attained, would lend a charm to the landscape-garden immeasurably surpassing that which a merely *human* interest could bestow. The true poet, possessed of very unusual pecuniary resources, might possibly, while retaining the necessary idea of *art* or *interest* or *culture*, so imbue his designs at once with extent and novelty of Beauty, as to convey the sentiment of *spiritual* interference. It will be seen that, in bringing about such result, he secures all the advantages of *interest* or *design,* while relieving his work of all the harshness and technicality of Art. In the most rugged of wildernesses—in the most savage of the scenes of pure Nature— there is apparent the *art* of a Creator; yet is *this* art apparent only to reflection; in no respect has it the obvious force of a feeling. Now, if we imagine this sense of the Almighty Design to be *harmonized* in a measurable degree! if we suppose a landscape whose combined *strangeness,* vastness, definiteness, and magnificence, shall inspire the idea of culture, or care, or superintendence, on the part of intelligences superior yet akin to humanity—then the sentiment of *interest* is preserved, while the Art is made to assume the air of an intermediate or secondary Nature—a Nature which is not God, nor an emanation of God, but which still is Nature, in the sense that it is the handiwork of the angels that hover between man and God.''

It was in devoting his gigantic wealth to the practical embodiment of a vision such as this— in the free exercise in the open air, which resulted from personal direction of his plans—in the continuous and unceasing *object* which these plans afforded—in the high spirituality of the object itself—in the contempt of ambition which it enabled him more to feel than to affect—and, lastly, it was in the companionship and sympathy of a devoted wife, that Ellison thought to find, *and found,* an exemption from the ordinary cares of Humanity, with a far greater amount of positive happiness than ever glowed in the rapt day-dreams of De Staël.

THE ISLAND OF THE FAY

[Published in *Graham's Magazine*, June, 1841.]

Nullus enim locus sine genio est.—*Servius.*

"*La musique,*" says Marmontel, in those "Contes Moraux"* which in all our translations, we have insisted upon calling "Moral Tales," as if in mockery of their spirit—"*la musique est le seul des talens qui jouissent de lui-même; tous les autres veulent des temoins.*" He here confounds the pleasure derivable from sweet sounds with the capacity for creating them. No more than any other *talent,* is that for music susceptible of complete enjoyment, where there is no second party to appreciate its exercise. And it is only in common with other talents that it produces *effects* which may be fully enjoyed in solitude. The idea which the *raconteur* has either failed to entertain clearly, or has sacrificed in its expression to his national love of *point,* is, doubtless, the very tenable one that the higher order of music is the most thoroughly estimated when we are exclusively alone. The

* Moraux is here derived from *mœurs,* and its meaning is "*fashionable,*" or, more strictly, "of manners."

proposition, in this form, will be admitted at
once by those who love the lyre for its own sake,
and for its spiritual uses. But there is one
pleasure still within the reach of fallen mortality
—and perhaps only one—which owes even more
than does music to the accessory sentiment of seclusion. I mean the happiness experienced in
the contemplation of natural scenery. In truth,
the man who would behold aright the glory of
God upon earth must in solitude behold that
glory. To me, at least, the presence—not of
human life only, but of life in any other form
than that of the green things which grow upon
the soil and are voiceless—is a stain upon the
landscape—is at war with the genius of the
scene. I love, indeed, to regard the dark valleys, and the gray rocks, and the waters that
silently smile, and the forests that sigh in uneasy slumbers, and the proud watchful mountains that look down upon all,—I love to regard
these as themselves but the colossal members of
one vast animate and sentient whole—a whole
whose form (that of the sphere) is the most perfect and most inclusive of all; whose path is
among associate planets; whose meek hand-
maiden is the moon, whose mediate sovereign is
the sun; whose life is eternity; whose thought
is that of a God; whose enjoyment is knowledge;
whose destinies are lost in immensity; whose
cognizance of ourselves is akin with our own
cognizance of the *animalculæ* which infest the
brain—a being which we, in consequence, regard
as purely inanimate and material, much in the

same manner as these *animalculæ* must regard us.

Our telescopes and our mathematical investigations assure us on every hand—notwithstanding the cant of the more ignorant of the priesthood—that space, and therefore that bulk, is an important consideration in the eyes of the Almighty. The cycles in which the stars move are those best adapted for the evolution, without collision, of the greatest possible number of bodies. The forms of those bodies are accurately such as, within a given surface, to include the greatest possible amount of matter;—while the surfaces themselves are so disposed as to accommodate a denser population than could be accommodated on the same surfaces otherwise arranged. Nor is it any argument against bulk being an object with God, that space itself is infinite; for there may be an infinity of matter to fill it. And since we see clearly that the endowment of matter with vitality is a principle—indeed, as far as our judgments extend, the *leading* principle in the operations of Deity,—it is scarcely logical to imagine it confined to the regions of the minute, where we daily trace it, and not extending to those of the august. As we find cycle within cycle without end,—yet all revolving around one far-distant centre which is the God-head, may we not analogically suppose in the same manner, life within life, the less within the greater, and all within the Spirit Divine? In short, we are madly erring, through self-esteem, in believing man, in either his tem-

poral or future destinies, to be of more moment
in the universe than that vast "clod of the valley" which he tills and contemns, and to which
he denies a soul for no more profound reason
than that he does not behold it in operation.*

These fancies, and such as these, have always
given to my mediations among the mountains
and the forests, by the rivers and the ocean, a
tinge of what the everyday world would not fail
to term fantastic. My wanderings amid such
scenes have been many, and far-searching, and
often solitary; and the interest with which I
have strayed through many a dim, deep valley,
or gazed into the reflected heaven of many a
bright lake, has been an interest greatly
deepened by the thought that I have strayed and
gazed *alone*. What flippant Frenchman† was
it who said in allusion to the well-known work
of Zimmerman, that, "*la solitude est une belle
chose; mais il faut quelqu'un pour vous dire
que la solitude est une belle chose?*" The epigram cannot be gainsaid; but the necessity is a
thing that does not exist.

It was during one of my lonely journeyings,
amid a far distant region of mountain locked
within mountain, and sad rivers and melancholy
tarns writhing or sleeping within all—that I
chanced upon a certain rivulet and island. I
came upon them suddenly in the leafy June, and
threw myself upon the turf, beneath the

* Speaking of the tides, Pomponius Mela, in his treatise
" *De Situ Orbis*," says " either the world is a great animal, or " etc.

† Balzac—in substance—I do not remember the words.

branches of an unknown odorous shrub, that I might doze as I contemplated the scene. I felt that thus only should I look upon it—such was the character of phantasm which it wore.

On all sides—save to the west, where the sun was about sinking—arose the verdant walls of the forest. The little river which turned sharply in its course, and was thus immediately lost to sight, seemed to have no exit from its prison, but to be absorbed by the deep green foliage of the trees to the east—while in the opposite quarter (so it appeared to me as I lay at length and glanced upward) there poured down noiselessly and continuously into the valley, a rich golden and crimson waterfall from the sunset fountains of the sky.

About midway in the short vista which my dreamy vision took in, one small circular island, profusely verdured, reposed upon the bosom of the stream.

> So blended bank and shadow there
> That each seemed pendulous in air—

so mirror-like was the glassy water, that it was scarcely possible to say at what point upon the slope of the emerald turf its crystal dominion began.

My position enabled me to include in a single view both the eastern and western extremities of the islet, and I observed a singularly marked difference in their aspects. The latter was all one radiant harem of garden beauties. It glowed and blushed beneath the eyes of the slant sunlight, and fairly laughed with flowers. The grass was short, springy, sweet-scented, and asphodel-interspersed. The trees were lithe, mirthful, erect—bright, slender, and graceful,—of Eastern figure and foliage, with bark smooth, glossy, and parti-colored. There seemed a deep sense of life and joy about all; and although no airs blew from out through the gentle sweepings to and fro of innumerable butterflies, that might have been mistaken for tulips with wings.*

The other or eastern end of the isle was whelmed in the blackest shade. A sombre, yet beautiful and peaceful gloom here pervaded all things. The trees were dark in color, and mournful in form and attitude, wreathing themselves into sad, solemn, and spectral shapes that conveyed ideas of mortal sorrow and untimely death. The grass wore the deep tint of the cypress, and the heads of its blades hung droopingly, and hither and thither among it were many small unsightly hillocks, low and narrow, and not very long, that had the aspect of graves, but were not; although over and all about them the rue and the rosemary clambered. The shade of the trees fell heavily upon the water, and seemed to bury itself therein, impregnating the depths of the element with darkness. I fancied that each shadow, as the sun descended lower and lower, separated itself sullenly from the trunk that gave it birth, and thus became absorbed by the stream; while other shadows issued moment-

---

* Florem putares nare per liquidum æthera.—*P. Commire.*

ly from the trees, taking the place of their predecessors thus entombed.

This idea, having once seized upon my fancy, greatly excited it, and I lost myself forthwith in revery. "If ever island were enchanted," said I to myself, "this is it. This is the haunt of the few gentle Fays who remain from the wreck of the race. Are these green tombs theirs?—or do they yield up their sweet lives as mankind yield up their own? In dying, do they not rather waste away mournfully, rendering unto God, little by little, their existence, as these trees render up shadow after shadow, exhausting their substance unto dissolution? What the wasting tree is to the water that imbibes its shade, growing thus blacker by what it preys upon, may not the life of the Fay be to the death which engulfs it?"

As I thus mused, with half-shut eyes, while the sun sank rapidly to rest, and eddying currents careered round and round the island, bearing upon their bosom large, dazzling, white flakes of the bark of the sycamore—flakes which, in their multiform positions upon the water, a quick imagination might have converted into anything it pleased,—while I thus mused, it appeared to me that the form of one of those very Fays about whom I had been pondering made its way slowly into the darkness from out the light at the western end of the island. She stood erect in a singularly fragile canoe, and urged it with the mere phantom of an oar. While within the influence of the lingering sunbeams, her attitude seemed indicative of joy—but sorrow deformed it as she passed within the shade. Slowly she glided along, and at length rounded the islet and reentered the region of light. "The revolution which has just been made by the Fay," continued I, musingly, "is the cycle of the brief year of her life. She has floated through her winter and through her summer. She is a year nearer unto death; for I did not fail to see that, as she came into the shade, her shadow fell from her, and was swallowed up in the dark water, making its blackness more black."

And again the boat appeared, and the Fay; but about the attitude of the latter there was more of care and uncertainty, and less of elastic joy. She floated again from out the light, and into the gloom (which deepened momently), and again her shadow fell from her into the ebony water, and became absorbed into its blackness. And again and again she made the circuit of the island, (while the sun rushed down to his slumbers), and at each issuing into the light, there was more sorrow about her person, while it grew feebler, and far fainter, and more indistinct; and at each passage into the gloom, there fell from her a darker shade, which became whelmed in a shadow more black. But at length, when the sun had utterly departed, the Fay, now the mere ghost of her former self, went disconsolately with her boat into the region of the ebony flood—and that she issued thence at all I cannot say, for darkness fell over all things, and I beheld her magical figure no more.

THE MASQUE OF THE RED DEATH

[Published in *Graham's Magazine,* May, 1842.]

THE "Red Death" had long devastated the country. No pestilence had ever been so fatal, or so hideous. Blood was its Avatar and its seal —the redness and the horror of blood. There were sharp pains, and sudden dizziness, and then profuse bleeding at the pores, with dissolution. The scarlet stains upon the body and especially upon the face of the victim, were the pest ban which shut him out from the aid and from the sympathy of his fellow-men. And the whole seizure, progress, and termination of the disease, were the incidents of half an hour.

But the Prince Prospero was happy and dauntless and sagacious. When his dominions were half depopulated, he summoned to his presence a thousand hale and light-hearted friends from among the knights and dames of his court, and with these retired to the deep seclusion of one of his castellated abbeys. This was an extensive and magnificent structure, the creation of the prince's own eccentric yet august taste. A strong and lofty wall girdled it in. This wall had gates of iron. The courtiers, having entered, brought furnaces and massy hammers and welded the bolts. They resolved to leave means neither of ingress or egress to the sudden impulses of despair or of frenzy from within. The abbey was amply provisioned. With such precautions the courtiers might bid defiance to contagion. The external world could take care of itself. In the meantime it was folly to grieve, or to think. The prince had provided all the appliances of pleasure. There were buffoons, there were improvisatori, there were ballet-dancers, there were musicians, there was Beauty, there was wine. All these and security were within. Without was the "Red Death."

It was toward the close of the fifth or sixth month of his seclusion, and while the pestilence raged most furiously abroad, that the Prince Prospero entertained his thousand friends at a masked ball of the most unusual magnificence.

It was a voluptuous scene, that masquerade. But first let me tell of the rooms in which it was held. There were seven—an imperial suite. In many palaces, however, such suites form a long and straight vista, while the folding doors slide back nearly to the walls on either hand, so that the view of the whole extent is scarcely impeded. Here the case was very different; as might have been expected from the duke's love of the *bizarre*. The apartments were so irregularly disposed that the vision embraced but little more than one at a time. There was a sharp turn at every twenty or thirty yards, and at each turn a novel effect. To the right and left, in the middle of each wall, a tall and narrow Gothic window looked out upon a closed corridor which pursued the windings of the suite. These windows were of stained glass whose color varied in accordance with the prevailing decorations of the chamber into which it opened. That at the eastern extremity was hung, for example in blue— and vividly blue were its windows. The second chamber was purple in its ornaments and tapestries, and here the panes were purple. The third was green throughout, and so were the casements. The fourth was furnished and lighted with orange—the fifth with white—the sixth with violet. The seventh apartment was closely shrouded in black velvet tapestries that hung all over the ceiling and down the walls, falling in heavy folds upon a carpet of the same material and hue. But in this chamber only, the color of the windows failed to correspond with the decorations. The panes here were scarlet—a deep blood color. Now in no one of the seven apartments was there any lamp or candelabrum, amid the profusion of golden ornaments that lay scattered to and fro or depended from the roof. There was no light of any kind emanating from lamp or candle within the suite of chambers. But in the corridors that followed the suite, there stood, opposite to each window, a heavy tripod, bearing a brazier of fire, that projected its rays through the tinted glass and so glaringly illumined the room. And thus were produced a multitude of gaudy and fantastic appearances. But in the western or black chamber the effect of the fire-light that streamed upon the dark hangings through the blood-tinted panes was ghastly in the extreme, and procured so wild a look upon the countenances of those who entered, that there were few of the company bold enough to set foot within its precincts at all.

It was in this apartment, also, that there stood against the western wall, a gigantic clock of ebony. Its pendulum swung to and fro with a dull, heavy monotonous clang; and when the minute hand made the circuit of the face, and the hour was to be stricken, there came from the brazen lungs of the clock a sound which was clear and loud and deep and exceedingly musical, but of so peculiar a note and emphasis that, at each lapse of an hour, the musicians of the orchestra were constrained to pause, momentarily, in their performance, to hearken to the sound; and thus the waltzers perforce ceased their evolutions; and there was a brief disconcert of the whole gay company; and, while the chimes of the clock yet rang, it was observed that the giddiest grew pale, and the more aged and sedate passed their hands over their brows as if in confused revery or meditation. But when the echoes had fully ceased, a light laughter at once pervaded the assembly; the musicians looked at each other and smiled as if at their own nervousness and folly, and made whispering vows, each to the other, that the next chiming of the clock should produce in them no similar emotion; and then after the lapse of sixty minutes (which embrace three thousand and six thousand seconds of the Time that flies), there came yet another chiming of the clock, and then were the same disconcert and tremulousness and meditation as before.

But, in spite of these things, it was a gay and magnificent revel. The tastes of the duke were peculiar. He had a fine eye for colors and effects. He disregarded the *decora* of mere fashion. His plans were bold and fiery, and his conceptions glowed with barbaric lustre. There are some who would have thought him mad. His followers felt that he was not. It was necessary to hear and see and touch him to be *sure* that he was not.

He had directed, in great part, the movable embellishments of the seven chambers, upon occasion of this great *fête;* and it was his own guiding taste which had given character to the masqueraders. Be sure they were grotesque. There were much glare and glitter and piquancy and phantasm—much of what has been since seen in ''Hernani.'' There were arabesque figures with unsuited limbs and appointments. There were delirious fancies such as the madman fashions. There were much of the beautiful, much of the wanton, much of the *bizarre,* something of the terrible, and not a little of that which might have excited disgust. To and fro in the seven chambers there stalked, in fact, a multitude of dreams. And these—the dreams—writhed in and about, taking hue from the rooms, and causing the wild music of the orchestra to seem as the echo of their steps. And, anon, there strikes the ebony clock which stands in the hall of the velvet. And then, for a moment, all is still, and all is silent save the voice of the clock. The dreams are stiff-frozen as they stand. But the echoes of the chime die away—they have endured but an instant—and a light, half-subdued laughter floats after them as they depart. And now again the music swells, and the dreams live, and writhe to and fro more merrily than ever, taking hue from the many-tinted windows through which stream the rays from the tripods. But to the chamber which lies most westwardly of the seven there are now none of the maskers who venture; for the night is waning away; and there flows a ruddier light through the blood-colored panes; and the blackness of the sable drapery appalls; and to him whose foot falls upon the sable carpet, there comes from the near clock of ebony a muffled peal more solemnly emphatic than any which reaches *their* ears who indulge in the more remote gaieties of the other apartments.

But these other apartments were densely crowded, and in them beat feverishly the heart of life. And the revel went whirlingly on, until at length there commenced the sounding of midnight upon the clock. And then the music ceased, as I have told; and the evolutions of the waltzers were quieted; and there was an uneasy cessation of all things as before. But now there were twelve strokes to be sounded by the bell of the clock; and thus it happened, perhaps that more

of thought crept, with more of time, into the
meditations of the thoughtful among those who
revelled. And thus too, it happened, perhaps,
that before the last echoes of the last chime had
utterly sunk into silence, there were many individuals in the crowd who had found leisure to
become aware of the presence of a masked figure
which had arrested the attention of no single individual before. And the rumor of this new
presence having spread itself whisperingly
around, there arose at length from the whole
company a buzz, or murmur, expressive of disap-
probation and surprise—then, finally, of terror,
of horror, and of disgust.

In an assembly of phantasms such as I have
painted, it may well be supposed that no ordinary appearance could have excited such sensation. In truth the masquerade license of the
night was nearly unlimited; but the figure in
question had out-Heroded Herod and gone beyond the bounds of even the prince's indefinite
decorum. There are chords in the hearts of the
most reckless which cannot be touched without
emotion. Even with the utterly lost, to whom
life and death are equally jests, there are matters
of which no jest can be made. The whole company, indeed, seemed now deeply to feel that in
the costume and bearing of the stranger neither
wit nor propriety existed. The figure was tall
and gaunt, and shrouded from head to foot in the
habiliments of the grave. The mask which concealed the visage was made so nearly to resemble
the countenance of a stiffened corpse that the

closest scrutiny must have had difficulty in detecting the cheat. And yet all this might have been endured, if not approved, by the mad revellers around. But the mummer had gone so far as to assume the type of the Red Death. His vesture was dabbled in *blood*—and his broad brow, with all the features of the face, was besprinkled with the scarlet horror.

When the eyes of Prince Prospero fell upon this spectral image (which, with a slow and solemn movement, as if more fully to sustain its *rôle,* stalked to and fro among the waltzers) he was seen to be convulsed,. in the first moment with a strong shudder either of terror or distaste; but, in the next, his brow reddened with rage.

"Who dares"—he demanded hoarsely of the courtiers who stood near him—"who dares insult us with this blasphemous mockery? Seize him and unmask him—that we may know whom we have to hang, at sunrise, from the battlements!"

It was in the eastern or blue chamber in which stood the Prince Prospero as he uttered these words. They rang throughout the seven rooms loudly and clearly, for the prince was a bold and robust man, and the music had become hushed at the waving of his hand.

It was in the blue room where stood the prince, with a group of pale courtiers by his side. At first, as he spoke, there was a slight rushing movement of this group in the direction of the intruder, who, at the moment was also near at hand, and now, with deliberate and stately step, made closer approach to the speaker. But from a certain nameless awe with which the mad assumptions of the mummer had inspired the whole party, there were found none who put forth hand to seize him; so that, unimpeded, he passed within a yard of the prince's person; and, while the vast assembly, as if with one impulse, shrank from the centres of the rooms to the walls, he made his way uninterruptedly, but with the same solemn and measured step which had distinguished him from the first, through the blue chamber to the purple—through the purple to the green—through the green to the orange—through this again to the white—and even thence to the violet, ere a decided movement had been made to arrest him. It was then, however, that the Prince Prospero, maddening with rage and the shame of his own momentary cowardice, rushed hurriedly through the six chambers, while none followed him on account of a deadly terror that had seized upon all. He bore aloft a drawn dagger, and had approached, in rapid impetuosity, to within three or four feet of the retreating figure, when the latter, having attained the extremity of the velvet apartment, turned suddenly and confronted his pursuer. There was a sharp cry—and the dagger dropped gleaming upon the sable carpet, upon which, instantly afterward, fell prostrate in death the Prince Prospero. Then, summoning the wild courage of despair, a throng of the revellers at once threw themselves into the black apartment, and, seizing the mummer, whose tall figure stood erect and motionless within the shadow of the ebony clock, gasped in unutterable horror at finding the grave cerements and corpse-like mask, which they handled with so violent a rudeness, untenanted by any tangible form.

And now was acknowledged the presence of the Red Death. He had come like a thief in the night. And one by one dropped the revellers in the blood-bedewed halls of their revel, and died each in the despairing posture of his fall. And the life of the ebony clock went out with that of the last of the gay. And the flames of the tripods expired. And Darkness and Decay and the Red Death held illimitable dominion over all.

KING PEST

A TALE CONTAINING AN ALLEGORY

[Published in the *Southern Literary Messenger*, September, 1835.]

> The gods do bear and well allow in kings
> The things which they abhor in rascal routes.
> —*Buckhurst's Tragedy of Ferrex and Porrex.*

ABOUT twelve o'clock, one night in the month of October, and during the chivalrous reign of the third Edward, two seamen belonging to the crew of the "Free and Easy," a trading schooner plying between Sluys and the Thames, and then at anchor in that river, were much astonished to find themselves seated in the tap-room of an ale-house in the parish of St. Andrews, London—which ale-house bore for sign the portraiture of a "Jolly Tar."

The room, although ill-contrived, smoke-blackened, low-pitched, and in every other respect agreeing with the general character of such places at the period—was nevertheless, in the opinion of the grotesque groups scattered here and there within it, sufficiently well adapted to its purpose.

VII. 6

Of these groups our two seamen formed, I think, the most interesting, if not the most conspicuous.

The one who appeared to be the elder, and whom his companion addressed by the characteristic appellation of "Legs," was at the same time much the taller of the two. He might have measured six feet and a half, and an habitual stoop in the shoulders seemed to have been the necessary consequence of an altitude so enormous. Superfluities in height were, however, more than accounted for by deficiencies in other respects. He was exceedingly thin; and might, as his associates asserted, have answered, when drunk, for a pennant at the masthead, or, when sober, have served for a jibboom. But these jests, and others of a similar nature, had evidently produced, at no time, any effect upon the cachinnatory muscles of the tar. With high cheekbones, a large hawk-nose, retreating chin, fallen under-jaw, and huge protruding white eyes, the expression of his countenance, although tinged with a species of dogged indifference to matters and things in general, was not the less utterly solemn and serious beyond all attempts at imitation or description.

The younger seaman was, in all outward appearance, the converse of his companion. His stature could not have exceeded four feet. A pair of stumpy bow-legs supported his squat, unwieldy figure, while his unusually short and thick arms, **with** no ordinary fists at their extremities, **swung** off dangling from his sides like the fins of a sea-turtle. Small eyes, of no particular color, twinkled far back in his head. His nose remained buried in the mass of flesh which enveloped his round, full, and purple face: and his thick upper-lip rested upon the still thicker one beneath with an air of complacent self-satisfaction, much heightened by the owner's habit of licking them at intervals. He evidently regarded his tall shipmate with a feeling half-wondrous, half-quizzical; and stared up occasionally in his face as the red setting sun stares up at the crags of Ben Nevis.

Various and eventful, however, had been the peregrinations of the worthy couple in and about the different tap-houses of the neighborhood during the earlier hours of the night. Funds even the most ample, are not always everlasting: and it was with empty pockets our friends had ventured upon the present hostelrie.

At the precise period, then, when this history properly commences, Legs, and his fellow, Hugh Tarpaulin, sat, each with both elbows resting upon the large oaken table in the middle of the floor, and with a hand upon either cheek. They were eying, from behind a huge flagon of unpaid-for "humming-stuff," the portentous words, "No Chalk," which to their indignation and astonishment were scored over the doorway by means of that very mineral whose presence they purported to deny. Not that the gift of decyphering written characters—a gift among the commonalty of that day considered little less cabalistical than the art of inditing—could, in strict justice, have been laid to the charge of either disciple of the sea; but there lurch about the whole—which foreboded, in the formation of the letters—an indescribable lee-lurch about the whole—which foreboded, in the opinion of both seamen, a long run of dirty weather; and determined them at once, in the allegorical words of Legs himself, to "pump ship, clew up all sail, and scud before the wind."

Having accordingly disposed of what remained of the ale, and looped up the points of their short doublets, they finally made a bolt for the street. Although Tarpaulin rolled twice into the fireplace, mistaking it for the door, yet their escape was at length happily effected—and half after twelve o'clock found our heroes ripe for mischief, and running for life down a dark alley in the direction of St. Andrew's Stair, hotly pursued by the landlady of the "Jolly Tar."

At the epoch of this eventful tale, and periodically, for many years before and after, all England, but more especially the metropolis, resounded with the fearful cry of "Plague!" The city was in a great measure depopulated—and in those horrible regions, in the vicinity of the Thames, where, amid the dark, narrow, and filthy lanes and alleys, the Demon of Disease, was supposed to have had his nativity, Awe, Terror, and Superstition were alone to be found stalking abroad.

By authority of the king such districts were placed *under ban*, and all persons forbidden, under pain of death, to intrude upon their dismal solitude. Yet neither the mandate of the monarch, nor the huge barriers erected at the entrance of the streets, nor the prospect of that loathsome death which, with almost absolute certainty, overwhelmed the wretch whom no peril could deter from the adventure, prevented the unfurnished and untenanted dwellings from being stripped, by the hand of nightly rapine, of every article, such as iron, brass, or lead-work, which could in any manner be turned to a profitable account.

Above all, it was usually found, upon the annual winter opening of the barriers, that locks, bolts, and secret cellars had proved but slender protection to those rich stores of wines and liquors which, in consideration of the risk and trouble of removal, many of the numerous dealers having shops in the neighborhood had consented to trust, during the period of exile, to so insufficient a security.

But there were very few of the terror-stricken people who attributed these doings to the agency of human hands. Pest-spirits, plague-goblins, and fever-demons were the popular imps of mischief; and tales so blood-chilling were hourly told, that the whole mass of forbidden buildings was, at length, enveloped in terror as in a shroud, and the plunderer himself was often scared away by the horrors his own depredations had created; leaving the entire vast circuit of prohibited district to gloom, silence, pestilence, and death.

It was by one of the terrific barriers already

mentioned, and which indicated the region beyond to be under the Pest-ban, that, in scrambling down an alley, Legs and the worthy Hugh
Tarpaulin found their progress suddenly impeded. To return was out of the question, and
no time was to be lost, as their pursuers were
close upon their heels. With thoroughbred seamen to clamber up the roughly fashioned plank-
work was a trifle; and, maddened with the twofold excitement of exercise and liquor, they
leaped unhesitatingly down within the enclosure,
and holding on their drunken course with shouts
and yellings, were soon bewildered in its noisome
and intricate recesses.

Had they not, indeed, been intoxicated beyond
moral sense, their reeling footsteps must have
been palsied by the horrors of their situation.
The air was cold and misty. The paving-stones,
loosened from their beds, lay in wild disorder
amid the tall rank grass, which sprang up around
the feet and ankles. Fallen houses choked up
the streets. The most fetid and poisonous smells
everywhere prevailed;—and by the aid of that
ghastly light which, even at midnight, never
fails to emanate from a vapory and pestilential
atmosphere, might be discerned lying in the by-
paths and alleys, or rotting in the windowless
habitations, the carcass of many a nocturnal
plunderer arrested by the hand of the plague in
the very perpetration of his robbery.

But it lay not in the power of images, or sen-
sations, or impediments such as these, to stay the
course of men who, naturally brave, and at that

time especially, brimful of courage and of "humming-stuff," would have reeled, as straight as their condition might have permitted, undauntedly into the very jaws of Death. Onward —still onward stalked the grim Legs, making the desolate solemnity echo and re-echo with yells like the terrific war-whoop of the Indian; and onward, still onward rolled the dumpy Tarpaulin, hanging on to the doublet of his more active companion, and far surpassing the latter's most strenuous exertions in the way of vocal music, by bull-roarings *in basso*, from the profundity of his stentorian lungs.

They had now evidently reached the stronghold of the pestilence. Their way at every step or plunge grew more noisome and more horrible —the paths more narrow and more intricate. Huge stones and beams falling momently from the decaying roofs above them, gave evidence, by their sullen and heavy descent, of the vast height of the surrounding houses; and while actual exertion became necessary to force a passage through frequent heaps of rubbish, it was by no means seldom that the hand fell upon a skeleton or rested upon a more fleshy corpse.

Suddenly, as the seamen stumbled against the entrance of a tall and ghastly-looking building, a yell more than usually shrill from the throat of the excited Legs, was replied to from within, in a rapid succession of wild, laughter-like, and fiendish shrieks. Nothing daunted at sounds, which, of such a nature, at such a time, and in such a place, might have curdled the very blood in hearts less irrevocably on fire, the drunken couple rushed headlong against the door, burst it open, and staggered into the midst of things with a volley of curses.

The room within which they found themselves proved to be the shop of an undertaker; but an open trap-door, in a corner of the floor near the entrance, looked down upon a long range of wine-cellars, whose depths the occasional sound of bursting bottles proclaimed to be well-stored with their appropriate contents.

In the middle of the room stood a table—in the centre of which again arose a huge tub of what appeared to be punch. Bottles of various wines and cordials, together with jugs, pitchers, and flagons of every shape and quality, were scattered profusely upon the board. Around it, upon coffin-tressels, was seated a company of six. This company I will endeavor to delineate one by one.

Fronting the entrance, and elevated a little above his companions, sat a personage who appeared to be the president of the table. His stature was gaunt and tall, and Legs was confounded to behold in him a figure more emaciated than himself. His face was as yellow as saffron —but no feature excepting one alone, was sufficiently marked to merit a particular description. This one consisted in a forehead so unusually and hideously lofty, as to have the appearance of a bonnet or crown of flesh superadded upon the natural head. His mouth was puckered and dimpled into an expression of ghastly affability, and his eyes, as indeed the eyes of all at table, were glazed over with the fumes of intoxication. This gentleman was clothed from head to foot in a richly-embroidered black silk-velvet pall, wrapped negligently around his form after the fashion of a Spanish cloak. His head was stuck full of sable hearse-plumes, which he nodded to and fro with a jaunty and knowing air; and, in his right hand, he held a huge human thigh-bone, with which he appeared to have been just knocking down some member of the company for a song.

Opposite him, and with her back to the door, was a lady of no whit the less extraordinary character. Although quite as tall as the person just described, she had no right to complain of his unnatural emaciation. She was evidently in the last stage of a dropsy; and her figure resembled nearly that of the huge puncheon of October beer which stood, with the head driven in, close by her side, in a corner of the chamber. Her face was exceedingly round, red, and full; and the same peculiarity, or rather want of peculiarity, attached itself to her countenance, which I before mentioned in the case of the president—that is to say, only one feature of her face was sufficiently distinguished to need a separate characterization: indeed the acute Tarpaulin immediately observed that the same remark might have applied to each individual person of the party; every one of whom seemed to possess a monopoly of some particular portion of physiognomy. With the lady in question this portion

proved to be the mouth. Commencing at the
right ear, it swept with a terrific chasm to the left
—the short pendants which she wore in either
auricle continually bobbing into the aperture.
She made, however, every exertion to keep her
mouth closed and look dignified, in a dress consisting of a newly-starched and ironed shroud
coming up close under her chin, with a crimpled
ruffle of cambric muslin.

At her right hand sat a diminutive young lady
whom she appeared to patronize. This delicate
little creature, in the trembling of her wasted
fingers, in the livid hue of her lips, and in the
slight hectic spot which tinged her otherwise
leaden complexion, gave evident indications of a
galloping consumption. An air of extreme *haut
ton,* however, pervaded her whole appearance;
she wore in a graceful and *dégagé* manner, a
large and beautiful winding-sheet of the finest
India lawn; her hair hung in ringlets over her
neck; a soft smile played about her mouth; but
her nose, extremely long, thin, sinuous, flexible,
and pimpled, hung down far below her under-
lip, and, in spite of the delicate manner in which
she now and then moved it to one side or the
other with her tongue, gave to her countenance
a somewhat equivocal expression.

Over against her, and upon the left of the
dropsical lady, was seated a little puffy, wheez-
ing, and gouty old man, whose cheeks reposed
upon the shoulders of their owner, like two huge
bladders of Oporto wine. With his arms folded,
and with one bandaged leg deposited upon the

table, he seemed to think himself entitled to some consideration. He evidently prided himself much upon every inch of his personal appearance, but took more especial delight in calling attention to his gaudy-colored surtout. This, to say the truth, must have cost him no little money, and was made to fit him exceedingly well —being fashioned from one of the curiously embroidered silken covers appertaining to those glorious escutcheons which, in England and elsewhere, are customarily hung up, in some conspicuous place, upon the dwellings of departed aristocracy.

Next to him, and at the right hand of the president, was a gentleman in long white hose and cotton drawers. His frame shook, in a ridiculous manner, with a fit of what Tarpaulin called "the horrors." His jaws, which had been newly shaved, were tightly tied up by a bandage of muslin; and his arms being fastened in a similar way at the wrists, prevented him from helping himself too freely to the liquors upon the table; a precaution rendered necessary, in the opinion of Legs, by the peculiarly sottish and wine-bibbing cast of his visage. A pair of prodigious ears, nevertheless, which it was no doubt found impossible to confine, towered away into the atmosphere of the apartment, and were occasionally pricked up in a spasm, at the sound of the drawing of a cork.

Fronting him, sixthly and lastly, was situated a singularly stiff-looking personage, who being afflicted with paralysis, must, to speak seriously, have felt very ill at ease in his unaccommodating habiliments. He was habited, somewhat uniquely, in a new and handsome mahogany coffin. Its top or head-piece pressed upon the skull of the wearer, and extended over it in the fashion of a hood, giving to the entire face an air of indescribable interest. Arm-holes had been cut in the sides for the sake not more of elegance than of convenience; but the dress, nevertheless, prevented its proprietor from sitting as erect as his associates; and as he lay reclining against his tressel, at an angle of forty-five degrees, a pair of huge goggle eyes rolled up their awful whites toward the ceiling in absolute amazement at their own enormity.

Before each of the party lay a portion of a skull, which was used as a drinking-cup. Overhead was suspended a human skeleton, by means of a rope tied round one of the legs and fastened to a ring in the ceiling. The other limb, confined by no such fetter, stuck off from the body at right angles, causing the whole loose and rattling frame to dangle and twirl about at the caprice of every occasional puff of wind which found its way into the apartment. In the cranium of this hideous thing lay a quantity of ignited charcoal, which threw a fitful but vivid light over the entire scene; while coffins, and other wares appertaining to the shop of an undertaker, were piled high up around the room, and against the windows, preventing any ray from escaping into the street.

At sight of this extraordinary assembly, and

of their still more extraordinary paraphernalia, our two seamen did not conduct themselves with that degree of decorum which might have been expected. Legs, leaning against the wall near which he happened to be standing, dropped his lower jaw still lower than usual, and spread open his eyes to their fullest extent; while Hugh Tarpaulin, stooping down so as to bring his nose upon a level with the table, and spreading out a palm upon either knee, burst into a long, loud, and obstreperous roar of very ill-timed and immoderate laughter.

Without, however, taking offence at behavior so excessively rude, the tall president smiled very graciously upon the intruders—nodded to them in a dignified manner with his head of sable plumes—and, arising, took each by an arm, and led him to a seat which some others of the company had placed in the meantime for his accommodation. Legs to all this offered not the slightest resistance, but sat down as he was directed; while the gallant Hugh, removing his coffin-tressel from its station near the head of the table, to the vicinity of the little consumptive lady in the winding sheet, plumped down by her side in high glee, and pouring out a skull of red wine, quaffed it to their better acquaintance. But at this presumption the stiff gentleman in the coffin seemed exceedingly nettled; and serious consequences might have ensued, had not the president, rapping upon the table with his truncheon, diverted the attention of all present to the following speech:

"It becomes our duty upon the present happy occasion——"

"Avast there!" interrupted Legs, looking very serious, "avast there a bit, I say, and tell us who the devil ye all are, and what business ye have here, rigged off like the foul fiends, and swilling the snug blue ruin stowed away for the winter by my honest ship-mate, Will Wimble, the undertaker!"

At this unpardonable piece of ill-breeding, all the original company half-started to their feet, and uttered the same rapid succession of wild fiendish shrieks which had before caught the attention of the seamen. The president, however, was the first to recover his composure, and at length, turning to Legs with great dignity, recommenced:

"Most willingly will we gratify any reasonable curiosity on the part of guests so illustrious, unbidden though they be. Know then that in these dominions I am monarch, and here rule with undivided empire under the title of 'King Pest the First.'

"This apartment, which you no doubt profanely suppose to be the shop of Will Wimble the undertaker—a man whom we know not, and whose plebeian appellation has never before this night thwarted our royal ears—this apartment, I say, is the Dais-Chamber of our Palace, devoted to the councils of our kingdom, and to other sacred and lofty purposes.

"The noble lady who sits opposite is Queen Pest, our Serene Consort. The other exalted personages whom you behold are all of our family, and wear the insignia of the blood royal under the respective titles of 'His Grace the Arch Duke Pest-Iferous'—'His Grace the Duke Pest-Ilential'—'His Grace the Duke Tem-Pest'—and 'Her Serene Highness the Arch Duchess Ana-Pest.'

"As regards," continued he, "your demand of the business upon which we sit here in council, we might be pardoned for replying that it concerns, and concerns *alone*, our own private and regal interest, and is in no manner important to any other than ourself. But in consideration of those rights to which as guests and strangers you may feel yourselves entitled, we will furthermore explain that we are here this night, prepared by deep research and accurate investigation, to examine, analyze, and thoroughly determine the indefinable spirit—the incomprehensible qualities and nature—of those inestimable treasures of the palate, the wines, ales, and liquors of this goodly metropolis: by so doing to advance not more our own designs than the true welfare of that unearthly sovereign whose reign is over us all, whose dominions are unlimited, and whose name is 'Death.'

"Whose name is Davy Jones!" ejaculated Tarpaulin, helping the lady by his side to a skull of liqueur, and pouring out a second for himself.

"Profane varlet!" said the president, now turning his attention to the worthy Hugh, "profane and execrable wretch!—we have said, that in consideration of those rights which, even in thy filthy person, we feel no inclination to violate, we have condescended to make reply to thy rude and unreasonable inquiries. We nevertheless, for your unhallowed intrusion upon our councils, believe it our duty to mulct thee and thy companion in each a gallon of Black Strap— having imbibed which to the prosperity of our kingdom—at a single draught—and upon your bended knees—ye shall be forthwith free either to proceed upon your way, or remain and be admitted to the privileges of our table, according to your respective and individual pleasures.''

''It would be a matter of utter unpossibility,'' replied Legs, whom the assumption and dignity of King Pest the First had evidently inspired with some feelings of respect, and who arose and steadied himself by the table as he spoke—''it would, please your majesty, be a matter of utter unpossibility to stow away in my hold even one fourth part of that same liquor which your majesty has just mentioned. To say nothing of the stuffs placed on board in the forenoon by way of ballast, and not to mention the various ales and liqueurs shipped this evening at various seaports, I have, at present, a full cargo of 'humming-stuff' taken in and duly paid for at the sign of the 'Jolly Tar.' You will therefore, please your majesty, be so good as to take the will for the deed—for by no manner of means either can I or will I swallow another drop— least of all a drop of that villainous bilge-water that answers to the name of 'Black Strap.' ''

"Belay that!" interrupted Tarpaulin, astonished not more at the length of his companion's
speech than at the nature of his refusal—"Belay
that, you lubber!—and I say, Legs, none of your
palaver. *My* hull is still light, although I confess you yourself seem to be a little top-heavy;
and as far as the matter of your share of the
cargo, why rather than raise a squall I would
find stowage-room for it myself, but——"

"This proceeding," interposed the president,
"is by no means in accordance with the terms
of the mulct or sentence, which is in its nature
Median, and not to be altered or recalled. The
conditions we have imposed must be fulfilled to
the letter, and that without a moment's hesitation—in failure of which fulfilment we decree
that you do here be tied neck and heels together,
and duly drowned as rebels in yon hogshead of
October beer!"

"A sentence!—a sentence!—a righteous and
just sentence!—a glorious decree!—a most
worthy and upright, and holy condemnation!"
shouted the Pest family altogether. The king
elevated his forehead into innumerable wrinkles;
the gouty little old man puffed like a pair of
bellows; the lady of the winding-sheet waved
her nose to and fro; the gentleman in the cotton
drawers pricked up his ears; she of the shroud
gasped like a dying fish; and he of the coffin
looked stiff and rolled up his eyes.

"Ugh! ugh! ugh!" chuckled Tarpaulin, without heeding the general excitation, "ugh! ugh!
ugh! ugh! ugh! ugh! ugh!—ugh! ugh! ugh!—I

VII. 7

was saying," said he,—"I was saying when Mr. King Pest poked in his marlinspike, that as for the matter of two or three gallons more or less of Black Strap, it was a trifle to a tight sea-boat like myself not over-stowed—but when it comes to drinking the health of the Devil (whom God assoilzie) and going down upon my marrow-bones to his ill-favored majesty there, whom I know, as well as I know myself to be a sinner, to be nobody in the whole world but Tim Hurly-gurly the stage-player!—why! it's quite another guess sort of a thing, and utterly and altogether past my comprehension."

He was not allowed to finish this speech in tranquillity. At the name of Tim Hurlygurly the whole assembly leaped from their seats.

"Treason!" shouted his Majesty King Pest the First.

"Treason!" said the little man with the gout.

"Treason!" screamed the Arch Duchess Ana-Pest.

"Treason!" muttered the gentleman with his jaws tied up.

"Treason!" growled he of the coffin.

"Treason! treason!" shrieked her majesty of the mouth; and seizing by the hinder part of his breeches the unfortunate Tarpaulin, who had just commenced pouring out for himself a skull of liqueur, she lifted him high into the air, and let him fall without ceremony into the huge open puncheon of his beloved ale. Bobbing up and down, for a few seconds, like an apple in a bowl of toddy, he, at length, finally disappeared amid the whirlpool of foam which, in the already effervescent liquor, his struggles easily succeeded in creating.

Not tamely, however, did the tall seaman behold the discomfiture of his companion. Jostling King Pest through the open trap, the valiant Legs slammed the door down upon him with an oath, and strode toward the centre of the room. Here tearing down the skeleton which swung over the table, he laid it about him with so much energy and good-will that, as the last glimpses of light died away within the apartment, he succeeded in knocking out the brains of the little gentleman with the gout. Rushing then with all his force against the fatal hogshead full of October ale and Hugh Tarpaulin, he rolled it over and over in an instant. Out poured a deluge of liquor so fierce—so impetuous—so overwhelming—that the room was flooded from wall to wall—the loaded table was overturned—the tressels were thrown upon their backs—the tub of punch into the fire-place—and the ladies into hysterics. Piles of death-furniture floundered about. Jugs, pitchers, and carboys mingled promiscuously in the *melée,* and wicker flagons encountered desperately with bottles of junk. The man with the horrors was drowned upon the spot—the little stiff gentleman floated off in his coffin—and the victorious Legs, seizing by the waist the fat lady in the shroud, rushed out with her into the street, and made a bee-line for the "Free and Easy," followed under easy sail by the redoubtable Hugh Tarpaulin, who, having sneezed three or four times, panted and puffed after him with the Arch Duchess Ana-Pest.

THE THOUSAND-AND-SECOND TALE OF SCHEHERAZADE

[Published in *Godey's Lady's Book*, February, 1845.]

Truth is stranger than fiction.—*Old Saying.*

HAVING had occasion, lately, in the course of some Oriental investigations, to consult the "Tellmenow Isitsöornot," a work which (like the "Zohar" of Simeon Jochaides) is scarcely known at all, even in Europe; and which has never been quoted, to my knowledge, by any American—if we except, perhaps, the author of the "Curiosities of American Literature";—having had occasion, I say, to turn over some pages of the first-mentioned very remarkable work, I was not a little astonished to discover that the literary world has hitherto been strangely in error respecting the fate of the vizier's daughter, Scheherazade, as that fate is depicted in the "Arabian Nights"; and that the *dénouement* there given, if not altogether inaccurate, as far as it goes, is at least to blame in not having gone very much farther.

For full information on this interesting topic, I must refer the inquisitive reader to the "Isit-

söornot'' itself; but in the meantime, I shall be
pardoned for giving a summary of what I there
discovered.

It will be remembered, that, in the usual ver-
sion of the tales, a certain monarch having good
cause to be jealous of his queen, not only puts
her to death, but makes a vow, by his beard and
the prophet, to espouse each night the most beautiful maiden in his dominions, and the next
morning to deliver her up to the executioner.

Having fulfilled this vow for many years to
the letter, and with a religious punctuality and
method that conferred great credit upon him as
a man of devout feeling and excellent sense, he
was interrupted one afternoon (no doubt at his
prayers) by a visit from his grand vizier, to
whose daughter, it appears, there had occurred
an idea.

Her name was Scheherazade, and her idea was,
that she would either redeem the land from the
depopulating tax upon its beauty, or perish,
after the approved fashion of all heroines, in the
attempt.

Accordingly, and although we do not find it
to be leap-year (which makes the sacrifice more
meritorious), she deputes her father, the grand
vizier, to make an offer to the king of her hand.
This hand the king eagerly accepts—(he had
intended to take it at all events, and had put off
the matter from day to day, only through fear of
the vizier),—but, in accepting it now, he gives
all parties very distinctly to understand, that,
grand vizier or no grand vizier, he has not the

slightest design of giving up one iota of his vow
or of his privileges.   When, therefore, the fair
Scheherazade insisted upon marrying the king,
and did actually marry him despite her father's
excellent advice not to do any thing of the kind—
when she would and did marry him, I say, will I,
nill I, it was with her beautiful black eyes as
thoroughly open as the nature of the case would
allow.

It seems, however, that this politic damsel
(who had been reading Machiavelli beyond
doubt), had a very ingenious little plot in her
mind.   On the night of the wedding she con-
trived, upon I forget what specious pretence, to
have her sister occupy a couch sufficiently near
that of the royal pair to admit of easy conversation from bed to bed; and, a little before cock-
crowing, she took care to awaken the good monarch, her husband (who bore here none the worse
will because he intended to wring her neck on the
morrow),—she managed to awaken him, I say,
(although on account of a capital conscience
and an easy digestion, he slept well,) by the profound interest of a story (about a rat and a black
cat, I think) which she was narrating (all in an
undertone, of course) to her sister.   When the
day broke, it so happened that this history was
not altogether finished, and that Scheherazade, in
the nature of things could not finish it just then,
since it was high time for her to get up and be
bowstrung—a thing very little more pleasant
than hanging, only a trifle more genteel!

The king's curiosity, however, prevailing, I am

sorry to say, even over his sound religious principles, induced him for this once to postpone the fulfilment of his vow until next morning, for the purpose and with the hope of hearing that night how it fared in the end with the black cat (a black cat, I think it was) and the rat.

The night having arrived, however, the lady Scheherazade not only put the finishing stroke to the black cat and the rat (the rat was blue) but before she well knew what she was about, found herself deep in the intricacies of a narration, having reference (if I am not altogether mistaken) to a pink horse (with green wings) that went, in a violent manner, by clockwork, and was wound up with an indigo key. With this history the king was even more profoundly interested than with the other—and, as the day broke before its conclusion (notwithstanding all the queen's endeavors to get through with it in time for the bowstringing), there was again no resource but to postpone that ceremony as before, for twenty-four hours. The next night there happened a similar accident with a similar result; and then the next—and then again the next; so that, in the end, the good monarch, having been unavoidably deprived of all opportunity to keep his vow during a period of no less than one thousand and one nights, either forgets it altogether by the expiration of this time, or gets himself absolved of it in the regular way, or (what is more probable) breaks it outright, as well as the head of his father confessor. At all events, Scheherazade, who, being lineally descended from Eve, fell heir, perhaps, to the whole seven baskets of talk, which the latter lady, we all know, picked up from under the trees in the Garden of Eden; Scheherazade, I say, finally triumphed, and the tariff upon beauty was repealed.

Now, this conclusion (which is that of the story as we have it upon record) is, no doubt, excessively proper and pleasant—but alas! like a great many pleasant things, is more pleasant than true; and I am indebted altogether to the "Isitsöornot" for the means of correcting the error. "*Le mieux*," says a French proverb, "*est l'ennemi du bien*," and, in mentioning that Scheherazade had inherited the seven baskets of talk, I should have added that she put them out at compound interest until they amounted to seventy-seven.

"My dear sister," said she, on the thousand-and-second night, (I quote the language of the "Isitsöornot" at this point, *verbatim*) "my dear sister," said she, "now that all this little difficulty about the bowstring has blown over, and that this odious tax is so happily repealed, I feel that I have been guilty of great indiscretion in withholding from you and the king (who I am sorry to say, snores—a thing no gentleman would do) the full conclusion of Sinbad the sailor. This person went through numerous other and more interesting adventures than those which I related; but the truth is, I felt sleepy on the particular night of their narration, and so was seduced into cutting them short—a grievous piece of misconduct, for which I only trust that Allah will forgive me. But even yet it is not too late to remedy my great neglect—and as soon as I have given the king a pinch or two in order to wake him up so far that he may stop making that horrible noise, I will forthwith entertain you (and him if he pleases) with the sequel of this very remarkable story.''

Hereupon the sister of Scheherazade, as I have it from the "Isitsöornot," expressed no very particular intensity of gratification; but the king, having been sufficiently pinched, at length ceased snoring, and finally said, "Hum!" and then "Hoo!" when the queen, understanding these words (which are no doubt Arabic) to signify that he was all attention, and would do his best not to snore any more—the queen, I say, having arranged these matters to her satisfaction, re-entered thus, at once, into the history of Sinbad the sailor:

"'At length, in my old age, (these are the words of Sinbad himself, as retailed by Scheherazade)—'at length, in my old age, and after enjoying many years of tranquillity at home, I became once more possessed of a desire of visiting foreign countries; and one day, without acquainting any of my family with my design, I packed up some bundles of such merchandise as was most precious and least bulky, and, engaging a porter to carry them, went with him down to the sea-shore, to await the arrival of any chance vessel that might convey me out of the kingdom into some region which I had not as yet explored.

"'Having deposited the packages upon the sands, we sat down beneath some trees, and looked out into the ocean in the hope of perceiving a ship, but during several hours we saw none whatever. At length I fancied that I could hear a singular buzzing or humming sound—and the porter, after listening awhile, declared that he also could distinguish it. Presently it grew louder, and then still louder, so that we could have no doubt that the object which caused it was approaching us. At length, on the edge of the horizon, we discovered a black speck, which rapidly increased in size until we made it out to be a vast monster, swimming with a great part of its body above the surface of the sea. It came toward us with inconceivable swiftness, throwing up huge waves of foam around its breast, and illuminating all that part of the sea through which it passed, with a long line of fire that extended far off into the distance.

"'As the thing drew near we saw it very distinctly. Its length was equal to that of three of the loftiest trees that grow, and it was as wide as the great hall of audience in your palace, O most sublime and munificent of the caliphs. Its body, which was unlike that of ordinary fishes, was as solid as a rock, and of a jetty blackness throughout all that portion of it which floated above the water with the exception of a narrow blood-red streak that completely begirdled it. The belly, which floated beneath the surface, and of which we could get only a glimpse now and then as the monster rose and fell with the billows, was entirely covered with metallic scales, of a color like that of the moon in misty weather. The back was flat and nearly white, and from it there extended upwards of six spines, about half the length of the whole body.

" 'This horrible creature had no mouth that we could perceive; but, as if to make up for this deficiency, it was provided with at least four score of eyes, that protruded from their sockets like those of the green dragon-fly, and were arranged all around the body in two rows, one above the other, and parallel to the blood-red streak, which seemed to answer the purpose of an eyebrow. Two or three of these dreadful eyes were much larger than the others, and had the appearance of solid gold.

" 'Although this beast approached us, as I have before said, with the greatest rapidity, it must have been moved altogether by necromancy —for it had neither fins like a fish nor web-feet like a duck, nor wings like the sea-shell which is blown along in the manner of a vessel; nor yet did it writhe itself forward as do the eels. Its head and its tail were shaped precisely alike, only, not far from the latter were two small holes that served for nostrils, and through which the monster puffed out its thick breath with prodigious violence, and with a shrieking, disagreeable noise.

" 'Our terror at beholding this hideous thing was very great, but it was even surpassed by our astonishment, when upon getting a nearer look, we perceived upon the creature's back a vast number of animals about the size and shape of men, and altogether much resembling them, except that they wore no garments (as men do), being supplied (by nature, no doubt,) with an ugly uncomfortable covering, a good deal like cloth but fitting so tight to the skin as to render the poor wretches laughably awkward, and put them apparently to severe pain. On the very tips of their heads were certain square-looking boxes, which, at first sight, I thought might have been intended to answer as turbans, but I soon discovered that they were excessively heavy and solid, and I therefore concluded they were contrivances designed by their great weight, to keep the heads of the animals steady and safe upon their shoulders. Around the necks of the creatures were fastened black collars, (badges of servitude, no doubt,) such as we keep on our dogs, only much wider and infinitely stiffer—so that it was quite impossible for these poor victims to move their heads in any direction without moving the body at the same time; and thus they were doomed to perpetual contemplation of their noses—a view puggish and snubby in a wonderful if not positively in an awful degree.

"'When the monster had nearly reached the shore where we stood, it suddenly pushed out one of its eyes to a great extent, and emitted from it a terrible flash of fire, accompanied by a dense cloud of smoke, and a noise that I can compare to nothing but thunder. As the smoke cleared away, we saw one of the odd man-animals standing near the head of the large beast with a trumpet in his hand, through which (putting it to his mouth) he presently addressed us in loud, harsh, and disagreeable accents, that, perhaps, we should have mistaken for language, had they not come altogether through the nose.

" 'Being thus evidently spoken to, I was at a loss how to reply, as I could in no manner understand what was said; and in this difficulty I turned to the porter, who was near swooning through affright, and demanded of him his opinion as to what species of monster it was, what it wanted, and what kind of creatures those were that so swarmed upon its back. To this the porter replied, as well as he could for trepidation, that he had once before heard of this sea-beast; that it was a cruel demon, with bowels of sulphur and blood of fire, created by evil genii as the means of inflicting misery upon mankind; that the things upon its back were vermin, such as sometimes infest cats and dogs, only a little larger and more savage; and that these vermin had their uses, however evil—for, through the torture they caused the beast by their nibblings and stingings, it was goaded into that degree of wrath which was requisite to make it roar and commit ill, and so fulfil the vengeful and malicious designs of the wicked genii.

" 'This account determined me to take to my heels, and, without once even looking behind me, I ran at full speed up into the hills, while the porter ran equally fast, although nearly in an opposite direction, so that, by these means, he finally made his escape with my bundles, of which I have no doubt he took excellent care—although this is a point I cannot determine, as I do not remember that I ever beheld him again.

"'For myself, I was so hotly pursued by a swarm of the men-vermin (who had come to the shore in boats) that I was very soon overtaken, bound hand and foot, and conveyed to the beast, which immediately swam out again into the middle of the sea.

"'I now bitterly repented my folly in quitting a comfortable home to peril my life in such adventures at this; but regret being useless, I made the best of my condition, and exerted myself to secure the good-will of the man-animal that owned the trumpet, and who appeared to exercise authority over his fellows. I succeeded so well in this endeavor that, in a few days, the creature bestowed upon me various tokens of his favor, and in the end even went to the trouble of teaching me the rudiments of what it was vain enough to denominate its language; so that, at length, I was enabled to converse with it readily, and came to make it comprehend the ardent desire I had of seeing the world.

"'*Washish squashish squeak, Sinbad, hey-diddle diddle, grunt unt grumble, hiss, fiss, whiss,*' said he to me one day after dinner—but I beg a thousand pardons, I had forgotten that your majesty is not conversant with the dialect of the Cock-neighs (so the man-animals were called; I presume because their language formed the connecting link between that of the horse and that of the rooster). With your permission, I will translate. '*Washish squashish*,' and so forth:—that is to say, 'I am happy to find, my dear Sinbad, that you are really a very excellent fellow; we are now about doing a thing which is called circumnavigating the globe; and since you are so desirous of seeing the world, I will strain a point and give you a free passage upon the back of the beast.'"

When the Lady Scheherazade had proceeded thus far, relates the "Isitsöornot," the king turned over from his left side to his right, and said:

"It is, in fact, *very* surprising, my dear queen, that you omitted, hitherto, these latter adventures of Sinbad. Do you know I think them exceedingly entertaining and strange?"

The king having thus expressed himself, we are told, the fair Scheherazade resumed her history in the following words:

"Sinbad went on in this manner with his narrative—'I thanked the man-animal for its kindness, and soon found myself very much at home on the beast, which swam at a prodigious rate through the ocean; although the surface of the latter is, in that part of the world, by no means flat, but round like a pomegranate, so that we went—so to say—either up hill or down hill all the time.'"

"That, I think, was very singular," interrupted the king.

"Nevertheless, it is quite true," replied Scheherazade.

"I have my doubts," rejoined the king; "but, pray, be so good as to go on with the story."

"I will," said the queen. " 'The beast,' continued Sinbad, 'swam, as I have related, up hill and down hill, until, at length, we arrived at an island, many hundreds of miles in circumference, but which, nevertheless, had been built in the middle of the sea by a colony of little things like caterpillars.' "*

"Hum! " said the king.

" 'Leaving this island,' said Sinbad—(for Scheherazade, it must be understood, took no notice of her husband's ill-mannered ejaculation)—'leaving this island, we came to another where the forests were of solid stone, and so hard that they shivered to pieces the finest-tempered axes with which we endeavored to cut them down.' "†

---

* The coralites.

† " One of the most remarkable natural curiosities in Texas is a petrified forest, near the head of Pasigno river. It consists of several hundred trees, in an erect position, all turned to stone. Some trees, now growing, are partly petrified. This is a startling fact for natural philosophers, and must cause them to modify the existing theory of petrifaction."—*Kennedy.*

This account, at first discredited, has since been corroborated by the discovery of a completely petrified forest, near the head waters of the Chayenne, or Chienne river, which has its source in the Black Hills of the Rocky chain.

There is scarcely, perhaps, a spectacle on the surface of the globe more remarkable, either in a geological or picturesque point of view than that presented by the petrified forest, near Cairo. The traveller, having passed the tombs of the caliphs, just beyond the gates of the city, proceeds to the southward, nearly at right angles to the road across the desert to Suez, and after having travelled some ten miles up a low barren valley, covered with sand, gravel, and sea shells, fresh as if the tide had retired but yesterday, crosses a low range of sandhills, which has for some distance run parallel to his path. The scene now presented to him is beyond conception singular and desolate. A mass of fragments of trees, all con-

"Hum!" said the king, again; but Scheher-azade, paying him no attention, continued in the language of Sinbad.

" 'Passing beyond this last island, we reached a country where there was a cave that ran to the distance of thirty or forty miles within the bowels of the earth, and that contained a greater number of far more spacious and more magnificent palaces than are to be found in all Damascus and Bagdad. From the roofs of these palaces there hung myriads of gems, like diamonds, but larger than men; and in among the streets of towers and pyramids and temples, there flowed immense rivers as black as ebony, and swarming with fish that had no eyes.' "*

"Hum!" said the king.

" 'We then swam into a region of the sea where we found a lofty mountain, down whose sides there streamed torrents of melted metal, some of which were twelve miles wide and sixty

---

verted into stone, and when struck by his horse's hoof ringing like cast iron, is seen to extend itself for miles and miles around him, in the form of a decayed and prostrate forest. The wood is of a dark brown hue, but retains its form in perfection, the pieces being from one to fifteen feet in length, and from half a foot to three feet in thickness, strewed so closely together, as far as the eye can reach, that an Egyptian donkey can scarcely thread its way through amongst them, and so natural that, were it in Scotland or Ireland, it might pass without remark for some enormous drained bog, on which the exhumed trees lay rotting in the sun. The roots and rudiments of the branches are, in many cases, nearly perfect, and in some of the worm-holes eaten under the bark are readily recognizable. The most delicate of the sap vessels, and all the finer portions of the centre of the wood, are perfectly entire, and bear to be examined with the strongest magnifiers. The whole are so thoroughly silicified as to scratch glass and are capable of receiving the highest polish.—*Asiatic Magazine.*

* The Mammoth Cave of Kentucky.

miles long* while from an abyss on the summit, issued so vast a quantity of ashes that the sun was entirely blotted out from the heavens, and it became darker than the darkest midnight; so that when we were even at the distance of a hundred and fifty miles from the mountain, it was impossible to see the whitest object, however close we held it to our eyes.' ''†

"Hum!'' said the king.

"'After quitting this coast, the beast continued his voyage until we met with a land in which the nature of things seemed reversed—for we here saw a great lake, at the bottom of which, more than a hundred feet beneath the surface of the water, there flourished in full leaf a forest of tall and luxuriant trees.' ''‡

"Hoo!'' said the king.

"'Some hundred miles farther on brought us to a climate where the atmosphere was so

---

* In Iceland, 1783.

† "During the eruption of Hecla, in 1766, clouds of this kind produced such a degree of darkness that, at Glaumba, which is more than fifty leagues from the mountain, people could only find their way by groping. During the eruption of Vesuvius, in 1794, at Caserta, four leagues distant, people could only walk by the light of torches. On the first of May, 1812, a cloud of volcanic ashes and sand, coming from a volcano in the island of St. Vincent, covered the whole of Barbadoes, spreading over it so intense a darkness that, at midday, in the open air, one could not perceive the trees or other objects near him, or even a white handkerchief placed at the distance of six inches from the eye."—*Murray* [*Encyclopaedia of Geography*], p. 215, *Phil. edit.*

‡ "In the year 1790, in the Caraccas during an earthquake a portion of the granite soil sank and left a lake eight hundred yards in diameter, and from eighty to a hundred feet deep. It was a part of the forest of Aripao which sank, and the trees remained green for several months under the water." —*Murray* [*Encyclopaedia of Geography*], p. 221.

dense as to sustain iron or steel, just as our own does feathers.' ''*

"Fiddle de dee," said the king.

" 'Proceeding still in the same direction, we presently arrived at the most magnificent region in the whole world. Through it there meandered a glorious river for several thousands of miles. This river was of unspeakable depth, and of a transparency richer than that of amber. It was from three to six miles in width; and its banks, which arose on either side to twelve hundred feet in perpendicular height, were crowned with ever-blossoming trees, and perpetual sweet-scented flowers, that made the whole territory one gorgeous garden; but the name of this luxuriant land was the Kingdom of Horror, and to enter it was inevitable death.' ''†

"Humph!" said the king.

" 'We left this kingdom in great haste, and, after some days, came to another, where we were astonished to perceive myriads of monstrous animals with horns resembling scythes upon their heads. These hideous beasts dig for themselves vast caverns in the soil, of a funnel shape, and line the side of them with rocks, so disposed one upon the other that they fall instantly, when trodden upon by other animals, thus precipitating them into the monsters' dens, where their blood is immediately sucked, and

---

* The hardest steel ever manufactured may, under the action of a blow-pipe, be reduced to an impalpable powder, which will float readily in the atmospheric air.

† The region of the Niger. See *Simmond's " Colonial Magazine."*

their carcasses afterwards hurled contemptuous-
ly out to an immense distance from "the caverns
of death.' ' ' '"*

"Pooh!" said the king.

" 'Continuing our progress, we perceived a
district with vegetables that grew not upon any
soil, but in the air.† There were others that
sprang from the substance of other vegetables;‡
others that derived their substance from the
bodies of living animals;§ and then again, there
were others that glowed all over with intense
fire;‖ others that moved from place to place
at pleasure,¶ and what was still more wonderful, we discovered flowers that lived and

* The *Myrmeleon*—lion-ant. The term " monster " is equally
applicable to small abnormal things and to great, while such
epithets as " vast " are merely comparative. The cavern of
the myrmeleon is *vast* in comparison with the hole of the common red ant. A grain of silex is also a " rock."

† The *Epidendron, Flos Aeris*, of the family of the *Orchideœ*,
grows with merely the surface of its roots attached to a tree
or other object, from which it derives no nutriment—subsisting
altogether upon air.

‡ The *Parasites*, such as the wonderful *Rafflesia Arnaldii*.

§ *Schouw* advocates a class of plants that grow upon living
animals—the *Plantœ Epizoœ*. Of this class are the *Fuci* and
Algœ.
    Mr. J. B. Williams, of Salem, Mass., presented the " Na-
tional Institute," with an insect from New Zealand, with the
following description:—" ' *The Hotte*,' a decided caterpillar,
or worm, is found growing at the foot of the *Rata* tree, with
a plant growing out of its head. This most peculiar and most
extraordinary insect travels up both the *Rata* and *Perriri*
trees, and entering into the top, eats its way, perforating the
trunk of the tree until it reaches the root, it then comes out
of the root, and dies, or remains dormant, and the plant propa-
gates out of its head ; the body remains perfect and entire, of
a harder substance than when alive. From this insect the
natives make a coloring for tattooing."

‖ In mines and natural caves we find a species of cryptoga-
mous *fungus* that emits an intense phosphorescence.

    The orchis, scabius and valisneria.

breathed and moved their limbs at will, and had, moreover, the detestable passion of mankind for enslaving other creatures, and confining them in horrid and solitary prisons until the fulfillment of appointed tasks.' ''*

"Pshaw!" said the king.

" 'Quitting this land, we soon arrived at another in which the bees and the birds are mathematicians of such genius and erudition, that they give daily instructions in the science of geometry to the wise men of the empire. The king of the place having offered a reward for the solution of two very difficult problems, they were solved upon the spot—the one by the bees, and the other by the birds; but the king keeping their solution a secret, it was only after the most profound researches and labor, and

---

* "The corolla of this flower (*Aristolochia Clematitis*), which is tubular, but terminating upwards in a ligulate limb, is inflated into a globular figure at the base. The tubular part is internally beset with stiff hairs, pointing downwards. The globular part contains the pistil, which consists merely of a germen and stigma, together with the surrounding stamens. But the stamens, being shorter than even the germen, cannot discharge the pollen so as to throw it upon the stigma, as the flower stands always upright till after impregnation. And hence, without some additional and peculiar aid, the pollen must necessarily fall down to the bottom of the flower. Now, the aid that nature has furnished in this case, is that of the *Tiputa Pennicornis*, a small insect, which entering the tube of the corolla in quest of honey, descends to the bottom, and rummages about till it becomes quite covered with pollen; but not being able to force its way out again, owing to the downward position of the hairs, which converge to a point like the wires of a mouse-trap, and being somewhat impatient of its confinement, it brushes backwards and forwards, trying every corner, till, after repeatedly traversing the stigma, it covers it with pollen sufficient for its impregnation, in consequence of which the flower soon begins to droop, and the hairs to shrink to the sides of the tube, effecting an easy passage for the escape of the insect."—*Rev. P. Keith—" System of Physiological Botany."*

the writing of an infinity of big books, during a
long series of years, that the men-mathemati-
cians at length arrived at the identical solutions
which had been given upon the spot by the bees
and by the birds.' ''*

"Oh, my!" said the king.

"'We had scarcely lost sight of this empire
when we found ourselves close upon another,
from whose shores there flew over our heads a
flock of fowls a mile in breadth, and two hundred and forty miles long; so that, although
they flew a mile during every minute, it required
no less than four hours for the whole flock to
pass over us—in which there were several millions of millions of fowl.' ''†

"Oh fy!" said the king.

* The bees—ever since bees were—have been constructing
their cells with just such sides, in just such number, and at
just such inclinations, as it has been demonstrated (in a
problem involving the profoundest mathematical principles)
are the very sides, in the very number, and at the very angles,
which will afford the creatures the most room that is com-
patible with the greatest stability of structure.

During the latter part of the last century, the question
arose among mathematicians—" to determine the best form
that can be given to the sails of a windmill, according to their
varying distances from the revolving vanes, and likewise from
the centres of the revolution." This is an excessively complex
problem, for it is, in other words, to find the best possible
position at an infinity of varied distances, and at an infinity
of points on the arm. There were a thousand futile attempts
to answer the query on the part of the most illustrious mathematicians; and when, at length, an undeniable solution was
discovered, men found that the wings of a bird had given it
with absolute precision ever since the first bird had traversed
the air.

† He observed a flock of pigeons passing betwixt Frankfort
and the Indian territory, one mile at least in breadth; it took
up four hours in passing; which, at the rate of one mile per
minute, gives a length of 240 miles; and, supposing three
pigeons to each square yard, gives 2,230,272,000 pigeons.—
" Travels in Canada and the United States," by Lieut. F. Hall.

" 'No sooner had we got rid of these birds, which occasioned us great annoyance, than we were terrified by the appearance of a fowl of another kind, and infinitely larger than even the rocs which I met in my former voyages; for it was bigger than the biggest of the domes on your seraglio, oh, most Munificent of Caliphs. This terrible fowl had no head that we could perceive, but was fashioned entirely of belly, which was of a prodigious fatness and roundness, of a soft-looking substance, smooth, shining and striped with various colors. In its talons, the monster was bearing away to his eyrie in the heavens, a house from which it had knocked off the roof, and in the interior of which we distinctly saw human beings, who, beyond doubt, were in a state of frightful despair at the horrible fate which awaited them. We shouted with all our might, in the hope of frightening the bird into letting go of its prey; but it merely gave a snort or puff, as if of rage and then let fall upon our heads a heavy sack which proved to be filled with sand! ' "

"Stuff! " said the king.

" 'It was just after this adventure that we encountered a continent of immense extent and prodigious solidity, but which, nevertheless, was supported entirely upon the back of a sky-blue cow that had no fewer than four hundred horns.' "*

"*That*, now, I believe," said the king, " be-

* " The earth is upheld by a cow of a blue color, having horns four hundred in number."—*Sale's Koran.*

cause I have read something of the kind before, in a book.''

" 'We passed immediately beneath this continent, (swimming in between the legs of the cow), and, after some hours, found ourselves in a wonderful country indeed, which, I was informed by the man-animal, was his own native land, inhabited by things of his own species. This elevated the man-animal very much in my esteem, and in fact, I now began to feel ashamed of the contemptuous familiarity with which I had treated him; for I found that the man-animals in general were a nation of the most powerful magicians, who lived with worms in their brain,* which, no doubt, served to stimulate them by their painful writhings and wrigglings to the most miraculous efforts of imagination.' ''

"Nonsense!" said the king.

" 'Among the magicians, were domesticated several animals of very singular kinds; for example, there was a huge horse whose bones were iron, and whose blood was boiling water. In place of corn, he had black stones for his usual food; and yet, in spite of so hard a diet, he was so strong and swift that he could drag a load more weighty than the grandest temple in this city, at a rate surpassing that of the flight of most birds.' ''†

* " The *Entozoa,* or intestinal worms, have repeatedly been observed in the muscles, and in the cerebral substance of men."—*See Wyatt's Physiology,* p. 143.

† On the Great Western Railway, between London and Exeter, a speed of 71 miles per hour has been attained. A train weighing 90 tons was whirled from Puddington to Didcot (53 miles) in 51 minutes.

"Twattle!" said the king.

"'I saw, also, among these people a hen without feathers, but bigger than a camel; instead of flesh and bone she had iron and brick; her blood, like that of the horse, (to whom, in fact, she was nearly related,) was boiling water; and like him she ate nothing but wood or black stones. This hen brought forth very frequently, a hundred chickens in the day; and, after birth, they took up their residence for several weeks within the stomach of their mother.'"*

"Fal lal!" said the king.

"'One of this nation of mighty conjurors created a man out of brass, and wood, and leather, and endowed him with such ingenuity that he would have beaten at chess, all the race of mankind with the exception of the great Caliph, Haroun Alraschid.† Another of these magi constructed (of like material) a creature that put to shame even the genius of him who made it; for so great were its reasoning powers that, in a second, it performed calculations of so vast an extent that they would have required the united labor of fifty thousand fleshy men for a year.‡ But a still more wonderful conjuror fashioned for himself a mighty thing that was neither man nor beast, but which had brains of lead, intermixed with a black matter like pitch, and fingers that employed with such in-

---

* The *Eccalobeion*.
† Maelzel's Automaton Chess-player.
‡ Babbage's Calculating Machine.

credible speed and dexterity that it would have had no trouble in writing out twenty thousand copies of the Koran in an hour; and this with so exquisite a precision, that in all the copies there should not be found one to vary from another by the breadth of the finest hair. This thing was of prodigious strength, so that it erected or overthrew the mightiest empires at a breath; but its powers were exercised equally for evil and for good.' "

"Ridiculous!" said the king.

"'Among this nation of necromancers there was also one who had in his veins the blood of the salamanders; for he made no scruple of sitting down to smoke his chibouc in a red-hot oven until his dinner was thoroughly roasted upon its floor.* Another had the faculty of converting the common metals into gold, without even looking at them during the process.† Another had such a delicacy of touch that he made a wire so fine as to be invisible.‡ Another had such quickness of perception that he counted all the separate motions of an elastic body, while it was springing backward and forward at the rate of nine hundred millions of times in a second.' "§

"Absurd!" said the king.

* *Chabert,* and since him, a hundred others.

† The Electrotype.

‡ *Wollaston* made a platinum for the field of views in a telescope a wire one eighteen-thousandth part of an inch in thickness. It could be seen only by means of the microscope.

§ Newton demonstrated that the retina beneath the influence of the violet ray of the spectrum, vibrated 900,000,000 of times in a second.

" 'Another of these magicians, by means of a fluid that nobody ever yet saw, could make the corpses of his friends brandish their arms, kick out their legs, fight, or even get up and dance at his will.*   Another had cultivated his voice to so great an extent that he could have made himself heard from one end of the world to the other.†   Another had so long an arm that he could sit down in Damascus and indite a letter at Bagdad—or indeed at any distance whatsoever.‡   Another commanded the lightning to come down to him out of the heavens, and it came at his call; and served him for a plaything when it came.   Another took two loud sounds and out of them made a silence.   Another constructed a deep darkness out of two brilliant lights.§   Another made ice in a red-hot furnace.‖   Another

* The Voltaic pile.

† The Electro telegraph transmits intelligence instantaneously—at least so far as regards any distance upon the earth.

‡ The Electro Telegraph Printing Apparatus.

§ Common experiments in Natural Philosophy. If two red rays from two luminous points be admitted into a dark chamber so as to fall on a white surface, and differ in their length by 0.0000258 of an inch, their intensity is doubled. So also if the difference in length be any whole-number multiple of that fraction. A multiple by 2¼, 3¼, &c., gives an intensity equal to one ray only; but a multiple by 2½, 3½, &c., gives the result of total darkness. In violet rays similar effects arise when the difference in length is 0.000157 of an inch; and with all other rays the results are the same—the difference varying with a uniform increase from the violet to the red.

Analogous experiments in respect to sound produce analogous results.

‖ Place a platina crucible over a spirit lamp, and keep it a red heat; pour in some sulphuric acid, which, though the most volatile of bodies at a common temperature, will be found to become completely fixed in a hot crucible, and not a drop evaporates—being surrounded by an atmosphere of its own, directed the sun to paint his portrait, and the sun did.* Another took this luminary with the moon and the planets, and having first weighed them with scrupulous accuracy, probed into their depths and found out the solidity of the substance of which they are made. But the whole nation is, indeed, of so surprising a necromantic ability, that not even their infants, nor their commonest cats and dogs have any difficulty in seeing objects that do not exist at all, or that for twenty millions of years before the birth of the nation itself, had been blotted out from the face of creation.' "†

"Preposterous!" said the king.

" 'The wives and daughters of these incomparably great and wise magi,' " continued Scheherazade, without being in any manner disturbed

it does not, in fact, touch the sides. A few drops of water are now introduced, when the acid, immediately coming in contact with the heated sides of the crucible, flies off in sulphurous acid vapor, and so rapid is its progress, that the caloric of the water passes off with it, which falls a lump of ice to the bottom; by taking advantage of the moment before it is allowed to re-melt, it may be turned out a lump of ice from a red-hot vessel.

* The Daguerreotype.

† Although light travels 167,000 miles in a second, the distance of 61 Cygni (the only star whose distance is ascertained) is so inconceivably great, that its rays would require more than ten years to reach the earth. For stars beyond this, 20—or even 1000 years—would be a moderate estimate. Thus, if they had been annihilated 20, or 1000 years ago, we might still see them to-day by the light which *started* from their surfaces 20 or 1000 years in the past time. That many which we see daily are really extinct, is not impossible—not even improbable.

The elder Herschel maintains that the light of the faintest nebulæ seen through his great telescope must have taken 3,000,000 years in reaching the earth. Some, made visible by Lord Ross' instrument, must, then, have required at least 20,000,000.

by these frequent and most ungentlemanly interruptions on the part of her husband—"'the wives and daughters of these eminent conjurers are every thing that is accomplished and refined; and would be every thing that is interesting and beautiful, but for an unhappy fatality that besets them, and from which not even the miraculous powers of their husbands and fathers has, hitherto, been adequate to save. Some fatalities come in certain shapes, and some in others—but this of which I speak has come in the shape of a crotchet.'"

"A what?" said the king.

"'A crotchet,'" said Scheherazade. "'One of the evil genii, who are perpetually upon the watch to inflict ill, has put it into the heads of these accomplished ladies that the thing which we describe as personal beauty consists altogether in the protuberance of the region which lies not very far below the small of the back. Perfection of loveliness, they say, is in the direct ratio of the extent of this lump. Having been long possessed of this idea, and bolsters being cheap in that country, the days have long gone by since it was possible to distinguish a woman from a dromedary——'"

"Stop!" said the king—"I can't stand that, and I won't. You have already given me a dreadful headache with your lies. The day, too, I perceive, is beginning to break. How long have we been married?——my conscience is getting to be troublesome again. And then that dromedary touch—do you take me for a fool? Upon the whole, you might as well get up and be throttled.''

These words, as I learn from the ''Isitsöornot,'' both grieved and astonished Scheherazade; but, as she knew the king to be a man of scrupulous integrity, and quite unlikely to forfeit his word, she submitted to her fate with a good grace. She derived, however, great consolation, (during the tightening of the bow-string,) from the reflection that much of the history remained still untold, and that the petulance of her brute of a husband had reaped for him a most righteous reward, in depriving him of many inconceivable adventures.

E. A. Poe.

FOUR BEASTS IN ONE

THE HOMO-CAMELEOPARD

[Published in the *Southern Literary Messenger,* March, 1836.]

Chacun a ses vertus.
—*Crébillon's Xerxes.*

ANTIOCHUS EPIPHANES is very generally looked upon as the Gog of the prophet Ezekiel. This honor is, however, more properly attributable to Cambyses, the son of Cyrus. And, indeed, the character of the Syrian monarch does by no means stand in need of any adventitious embellishment. His accession to the throne, or rather his usurpation of the sovereignty, a hundred and seventy-one years before the coming of Christ; his attempt to plunder the temple of Diana at Ephesus; his implacable hostility to the Jews; his pollution of the Holy of Holies; and his miserable death at Taba, after a tumultuous reign of eleven years, are circumstances of a prominent kind, and therefore more generally noticed by the historians of his time than the impious, dastardly, cruel, silly, and whimsical achievements which make up the sum total of his private life and reputation.

*   *   *   *   *   *   *

Let us suppose, gentle reader, that it is now the year of the world three thousand eight hundred and thirty, and let us, for a few minutes, imagine ourselves at that most grotesque habitation of man, the remarkable city of Antioch. To be sure there were, in Syria and other countries, sixteen cities of that appellation, besides the one to which I more particularly allude. But *ours* is that which went by the name of Antiochia Epidaphne, from its vicinity to the little village of Daphne, where stood a temple to that divinity. It was built (although about this matter there is some dispute) by Seleucus Nicanor, the first king of the country after Alexander the Great, in memory of his father Antiochus, and became immediately the residence of the Syrian monarchy. In the flourishing times of the Roman Empire it was the ordinary station of the prefect of the eastern provinces; and many of the emperors of the Queen city (among whom may be mentioned, especially, Verus and Valens) spent here the greater part of their time. But I perceive we have arrived at the city itself. Let us ascend this battlement, and throw our eyes upon the town and neighboring country.

"What broad and rapid river is that which forces its way, with innumerable falls, through the mountainous wilderness, and finally through the wilderness of buildings?"

VII. 9

That is the Orontes, and it is the only water in sight, with the exception of the Mediterranean, which stretches, like a broad mirror, about twelve miles off to the southward. Every one has seen the Mediterranean; but let me tell you, there are few who have had a peep at Antioch. By few, I mean, few who, like you and me, have had, at the same time, the advantages of a modern education. Therefore cease to regard that sea, and give your whole attention to the mass of houses that lie beneath us. You will remember that it is now the year of the world three thousand eight hundred and thirty. Were it later—for example, were it the year of our Lord eighteen hundred and forty-five—we should be deprived of this extraordinary spectacle. In the nineteenth century Antioch is—that is to say, Antioch *will* be—in a lamentable state of decay. It will have been, by that time, totally destroyed, at three different periods, by three successive earthquakes. Indeed, to say the truth, what little of its former self may then remain, will be found in so desolate and ruinous a state that the patriarch shall have removed his residence to Damascus. This is well. I see you profit by my advice, and are making the most of your time in inspecting the premises—in

> —satisfying your eyes
> With the memorials and the things of fame
> That most renown this city.—

I beg pardon; I had forgotten that Shakespeare will not flourish for seventeen hundred and fifty years to come. But does not the appearance of Epidaphne justify me in calling it *grotesque?*

"It is well fortified; and in this respect is as much indebted to nature as to art."

Very true.

"There are a prodigious number of stately palaces."

There are.

"And the numerous temples, sumptuous and magnificent, may bear comparison with the most lauded of antiquity."

All this I must acknowledge. Still there is an infinity of mud huts, and abominable hovels. We cannot help perceiving abundance of filth in every kennel, and, were it not for the overpowering fumes of idolatrous incense, I have no doubt we should find a most intolerable stench. Did you ever behold streets so insufferably narrow, or houses so miraculously tall? What a gloom their shadows cast upon the ground! It is well the swinging lamps in those endless colonnades are kept burning throughout the day; we should otherwise have the darkness of Egypt in the time of her desolation.

"It is certainly a strange place! What is the meaning of yonder singular building? See! it towers above all others, and lies to the eastward of what I take to be the royal palace!"

That is the new Temple of the Sun, who is adored in Syria under the title of Elah Gabalah. Hereafter a very notorious Roman emperor will institute this worship in Rome, and thence derive a cognomen, Heliogabalus. I dare say you would like to take a peep at the divinity of the temple. You need not look up at the heavens; his Sunship is not there—at least not the Sunship adored by the Syrians. *That* deity will be found in the interior of yonder building. He is worshipped under the figure of a large stone pillar terminating at the summit in a cone or *pyramid*, whereby is denoted Fire.

"Hark!—behold!—who *can* those ridiculous beings be, half naked, with their faces painted, shouting and gesticulating to the rabble?"

Some few are mountebanks. Others more particularly belong to the race of philosophers. The greatest portion, however—those especially who belabor the populace with clubs—are the principal courtiers of the palace, executing, as in duty bound, some laudable comicality of the king's.

"But what have we here? Heavens! the town is swarming with wild beasts! How terrible a spectacle!—how dangerous a peculiarity!"

Terrible if you please; but not in the least degree dangerous. Each animal, if you will take the pains to observe, is following, very quietly, in the wake of its master. Some few, to be sure, are led with a rope about the neck, but these are chiefly the lesser or timid species. The lion, the tiger, and the leopard are entirely without restraint. They have been trained without difficulty to their present profession, and attend upon their respective owners in the capacity of *valets-de-chambre*. It is true, there are occasions when Nature asserts her violated dominion:—

but then the devouring of a man-at-arms, or the throttling of a consecrated bull, is a circumstance of too little moment to be more than hinted at in Epidaphne.

"But what extraordinary tumult do I hear? Surely this is a loud noise even for Antioch! It argues some commotion of unusual interest."

Yes—undoubtedly. The king has ordered some novel spectacle—some gladiatorial exhibition at the hippodrome—or perhaps the massacre of the Scythian prisoners—or the conflagration of his new palace—or the tearing down of a handsome temple—or, indeed, a bonfire of a few Jews. The uproar increases. Shouts of laughter ascend the skies. The air becomes dissonant with wind instruments, and horrible with the clamor of a million throats. Let us descend, for the love of fun, and see what is going on! This way—be careful! Here we are in the principal street, which is called the street of Timarchus. The sea of people is coming this way, and we shall find a difficulty in stemming the tide. They are pouring through the alley of Heraclides, which leads directly from the palace—therefore the king is most probably among the rioters. Yes—I hear the shouts of the herald proclaiming his approach in the pompous phraseology of the East. We shall have a glimpse of his person as he passes by the temple of Ashimah. Let us ensconce ourselves in the vestibule of the sanctuary; he will be here anon. In the meantime let us survey this image. What is it? Oh! it is the god Ashimah in proper person. You perceive, however, that he is neither a lamb, nor a goat, nor a satyr; neither has he much resemblance to the Pan of the Arcadians. Yet all these appearances have been given—I beg pardon—*will* be given—by the learned of future ages, to the Ashimah of the Syrians. Put on your spectacles, and tell me what it is. What is it?

"Bless me! it is an ape!"

True—a baboon; but by no means the less a deity. His name is a derivation of the Greek *Simia*—what great fools are antiquarians! But see!—see!—yonder scampers a ragged little urchin. Where is he going? What is he bawling about? What does he say? Oh! he says the king is coming in triumph; that he is dressed in state; that he has just finished putting to death, with his own hand, a thousand chained Israelitish prisoners! For this exploit the ragamuffin is lauding him to the skies! Hark! here comes a troop of a similar description. They have made a Latin hymn upon the valor of the king, and are singing it as they go:

Mille, mille, mille,
Mille, mille, mille,
Decollavimus, unus homo!
Mille, mille, mille, mille, decollavimus!
Mille, mille, mille,
Vivat qui mille mille occidit!
Tantum vini habet nemo
Quantum sanguinis effudit! *

* Flavius Vospicus says, that the hymn here introduced was sung by the rabble upon the occasion of Aurelian, in the Sarmatic war, having slain, with his own hand, nine hundred and fifty of the enemy.

Which may be thus paraphrased:

A thousand, a thousand, a thousand,
A thousand, a thousand, a thousand,
We, with one warrior, have slain!
A thousand, a thousand, a thousand, a thousand.
    Sing a thousand over again!
        Soho!—let us sing
        Long life to our king,
    Who knocked over a thousand so fine!
        Soho!—let us roar,
        He has given us more
Than all Syria can furnish of wine!

"Do you hear that flourish of trumpets?"

Yes—the king is coming! See! the people are aghast with admiration, and lift up their eyes to the heavens in reverence! He comes!—he is coming!—there he is!

"Who?—where?—the king?—I do not behold him;—cannot say that I perceive him."

Then you must be blind.

"Very possible. Still I see nothing but a tumultuous mob of idiots and madmen, who are busy in prostrating themselves before a gigantic cameleopard, and endeavoring to obtain a kiss of the animal's hoofs. See! the beast has very justly kicked one of the rabble over—and another—and another—and another. Indeed, I cannot help admiring the animal for the excellent use he is making of his feet."

Rabble, indeed!—why these are the noble and free citizens of Epidaphne! Beast, did you say? —take care that you are not overheard. Do you not perceive that the animal has the visage of a man? Why, my dear sir, that cameleopard is no other than Antiochus Epiphanes—Antiochus the Illustrious, King of Syria, and the most potent of all the autocrats of the East! It is true, that he is entitled, at times, Antiochus Epimanes—Antiochus the madman—but that is because all people have not the capacity to appreciate his merits. It is also certain that he is at present ensconced in the hide of a beast, and is doing his best to play the part of a cameleopard; but this is done for the better sustaining his dignity as king. Besides, the monarch is of gigantic stature, and the dress is therefore neither unbecoming nor over large. We may, however, presume he would not have adopted it but for some occasion of especial state. Such, you will allow, is the massacre of a thousand Jews. With how superior a dignity the monarch perambulates on all fours! His tail, you perceive, is held aloft by his two principal concubines, Elline and Argelais; and his whole appearance would be infinitely prepossessing, were it not for the protuberance of his eyes, which will certainly start out of his head, and the queer color of his face, which has become nondescript from the quantity of wine he had swallowed. Let us follow him to the hippodrome, whither he is proceeding, and listen to the song of triumph which he is commencing:

> Who is king but Epiphanes?
> Say—do you know?
> Who is king but Epiphanes?
> Bravo!—bravo!
> There is none but Epiphanes,
> No—there is none;
> So tear down the temples,
> And put out the sun!

Well and strenuously sung! The populace are hailing him "Prince of Poets," as well as "Glory of the East," "Delight of the Universe," and "Most remarkable of Cameleopards." They have *encored* his effusion, and—do you hear?—he is singing it over again. When he arrives at the hippodrome, he will be crowned with the poetic wreath, in anticipation of his victory at the approaching Olympics.

"But, good Jupiter! what is the matter in the crowd behind us?"

Behind us, did you say?—oh! ah!—I perceive. My friend, it is well that you spoke in time. Let us get into a place of safety as soon as possible. Here!—let us conceal ourselves in the arch of this aqueduct, and I will inform you presently of the origin of the commotion. It has turned out as I have been anticipating. The singular appearance of the cameleopard with the head of a man, has, it seems, given offence to the notions of propriety entertained in general by the wild animals domesticated in the city. A mutiny has been the result; and, as is usual upon such occasions, all human efforts will be of no avail in quelling the mob. Several of the Syrians have already been devoured; but the general voice of the four-footed patriots seems to be for eating up the cameleopard. "The Prince of Poets," therefore, is upon his hinder legs running for his life. His courtiers have left him in the lurch, and his concubines have followed so excellent an example. "Delight of the Universe," thou art in a sad predicament! "Glory of the East,"

thou art in danger of mastication! Therefore
never regard so piteously thy tail; it will undoubtedly be draggled in the mud, and for this
there is no help. Look not behind thee, then, at
its unavoidable degradation; but take courage,
ply thy legs with vigor, and scud for the hippodrome! Remember that thou art Antiochus
Epiphanes. Antiochus the Illustrious!—also
"Prince of Poets," "Glory of the East," "Delight of the Universe," and "Most Remarkable
of Cameleopards!" Heavens! what a power of
speed thou art displaying! What a capacity for
leg-bail thou art developing! Run, Prince!—
Bravo, Epiphanes!—Well done, Cameleopard!—
Glorious Antiochus!—He runs!—he leaps!—he
flies! Like an arrow from a catapult he approaches the hippodrome! He leaps!—he
shrieks!—he·is there! This is well; for hadst
thou, "Glory of the East," been half a second
longer in reaching the gates of the amphitheatre,
there is not a bear's cub in Epidaphne that
would not have had a nibble at thy carcass. Let
us be off—let us take our departure!—for we
shall find our delicate modern ears unable to en-
dure the vast uproar which is about to commence
in celebration of the king's escape! Listen! it
has already commenced. See!—the whole town
is topsy-turvy.

"Surely this is the most populous city of the
East! What a wilderness of people! What a
jumble of all ranks and ages! What a multi-
plicity of sects and nations! what a variety of
costumes! what a Babel of languages! what a

screaming of beasts! what a tinkling of instruments! what a parcel of philosophers!"

Come let us be off.

"Stay a moment! I see a vast hubbub in the hippodrome; what is the meaning of it, I beseech you?"

That?—oh, nothing! The noble and free citizens of Epidaphne being, as they declare, well satisfied of the faith, valor, wisdom, and divinity of their king, and having, moreover, been eyewitnesses of his late superhuman agility, do think it no more than their duty to invest his brows (in addition to the poetic crown) with the wreath of victory in the foot-race—a wreath which it is evident he *must* obtain at the celebration of the next Olympiad, and which, therefore, they now give him in advance.

A TALE OF JERUSALEM

[Published in the *Southern Literary Messenger*, April, 1836.]

Intonsos rigidam in frontem ascendere canos
Passus erat————
                        LUCAN——*De Catone.*

————a bristly *bore.*
                        Translation.

"LET us hurry to the walls," said Abel-Phittim to Buzi-Ben-Levi and Simeon the Pharisee, on the tenth day of the month Thammuz, in the year of the world three thousand nine hundred and forty-one—"let us hasten to the ramparts adjoining the gate of Benjamin, which is in the city of David, and overlooking the camp of the uncircumcised; for it is the last hour of the fourth watch, being sunrise; and the idolaters, in fulfilment of the promise of Pompey, should be awaiting us with the lambs for the sacrifices."

Simeon, Abel-Phittim, and Buzi-Ben-Levi, were the Gizbarim, or sub-collectors of the offering, in the holy city of Jerusalem.

"Verily," replied the Pharisee, "let us hasten: for this generosity in the heathen is unwonted; and fickle-mindedness has ever been an attribute of the worshippers of Baal."

"That they are fickle-minded and treacherous is as true as the Pentateuch," said Buzi-Ben-Levi, "but that is only toward the people of Adonai. When was it ever known that the Ammonites proved wanting to their own interests? Methinks it is no great stretch of generosity to allow us lands for the altar of the Lord receiving in lieu thereof thirty silver shekels per head!"

"Thou forgettest, however, Ben-Levi," replied Abel-Phittim, "that the Roman Pompey, who is now impiously besieging the city of the Most High, has no assurity that we apply not the lambs thus purchased for the altar, to the sustenance of the body, rather than of the spirit."

"Now, by the five corners of my beard!" shouted the Pharisee, who belonged to the sect called The Dashers (that little knot of saints whose manner of *dashing* and lacerating the feet against the pavement was long a thorn and a reproach to less zealous devotees—a stumbling-block to less gifted perambulators)—"by the five corners of that beard which, as a priest, I am forbidden to shave!—have we lived to see the day when a blaspheming and idolatrous upstart of Rome shall accuse us of appropriating to the appetites of the flesh the most holy and consecrated elements? Have we lived to see the day when"——

"Let us not question the motives of the Philistine," interrupted Abel-Phittim, "for to-day we profit for the first time by his avarice or by his generosity; but rather let us hurry to the ramparts, lest offerings should be wanting for that altar whose fire the rains of heaven cannot extinguish, and whose pillars of smoke no tempest can turn aside.''

That part of the city to which our worthy Gizbarim now hastened, and which bore the name of its architect, King David, was esteemed the most strongly fortified district of Jerusalem; being situated upon the steep and lofty hill of Zion. Here, a broad, deep, circumvallatory trench, hewn from the solid rock, was defended by a wall of great strength erected upon its inner edge. This wall was adorned, at regular interspaces, by square towers of white marble; the lowest sixty, and the highest one hundred and twenty cubits in height. But, in the vicinity of the gate of Benjamin, the wall arose by no means from the margin of the fosse. On the contrary, between the level of the ditch and the basement of the rampart, sprang up a perpendicular cliff of two hundred and fifty cubits, forming part of the precipitous Mount Moriah. So that when Simeon and his associates arrived on the summit of the tower called 'Adoni-Bezek—the loftiest of all the turrets around about Jerusalem, and the usual place of conference with the besieging army—they looked down upon the camp of the enemy from an eminence excelling by many feet that of the Pyramid of Cheops, and, by several, that of the temple of Belus.

''Verily,'' sighed the Pharisee, as he peered dizzily over the precipice, ''the uncircumcised

are as the sands by the seashore—as the locusts
in the wilderness! The valley of the King hath
become the valley of Adommin.''

"And yet," added Ben-Levi, "thou canst not
point me out a Philistine—no, not one—from
Aleph to Tau—from the wilderness to the battlements—who seemeth any bigger than the letter Jod!''

"Lower away the basket with the shekels of
silver!'' here shouted a Roman soldier in a
hoarse, rough voice, which appeared to issue
from the regions of Pluto—"lower away the
basket with the accursed coin which it has broken
the jaw of a noble Roman to pronounce! Is it
thus you evince your gratitude to our master
Pompeius, who, in his condescension, has thought
fit to listen to your idolatrous importunities?
The god Phœbus, who is a true god, has been
charioted for an hour—and were you not to be on
the ramparts by sunrise? Ædepol! do you think
that we, the conquerors of the world, have nothing better to do than stand waiting by the walls
of every kennel, to traffic with the dogs of the
earth? Lower away! I say—and see that your
trumpery be bright in color and just in weight!''

"El Elohim!'' ejaculated the Pharisee, as the
discordant tones of the centurion rattled up the
crags of the precipice, and fainted away against
the temple—"El Elohim!—*who* is the God
Phœbus?—*whom* doth the blasphemer invoke?
Thou, Buzi-Ben-Levi! who art read in the laws
of the Gentiles, and hast sojourned among them
who dabble with the Teraphim!—is it Nergal of

whom the idolater speaketh?—or Ashimah?—or
Nibhaz?—or Tartak?—or Adramalech?—or
Anamalech?—or Succoth-Benith?—or Dagon?—
or Belial?—or Baal-Perith?—or Baal-Peor?—or
Baal-Zebub?''

''Verily it is neither—but beware how thou
lettest the rope slip too rapidly through thy
fingers; for should the wicker-work chance to
hang on the projection of yonder crag, there will
be a woful outpouring of the holy things of the
sanctuary.''

By the assistance of some rudely constructed
machinery, the heavily laden basket was now
carefully lowered down among the multitude;
and, from the giddy pinnacle, the Romans were
seen gathering confusedly round it; but owing
to the vast height and the prevalence of a fog,
no distinct view of their operations could be obtained.

Half an hour had already elapsed.

''We shall be too late!'' sighed the Pharisee,
as at the expiration of this period, he looked over
into the abyss—''we shall be too late! we shall be
turned out of office by the Katholim.''

''No more,'' responded Abel-Phittim,—''no
more shall we feast upon the fat of the land—no
longer shall our beards be odorous with frank-
incense—our loins girded up with fine linen from
the Temple.''

''Raca!'' swore Ben-Levi, ''Raca! do they
mean to defraud us of the purchase money? or,
Holy Moses! are they weighing the shekels of the
tabernacle?''

"They have given the signal at last!" cried the Pharisee—"they have given the signal at last!—pull away, Abel-Phittim!—and thou, Buzi-Ben-Levi, pull away!—for verily the Philistines have either still hold upon the basket, or the Lord hath softened their hearts to place therein a beast of good weight!" And the Gizbarim pulled away, while their burthen swung heavily upward through the still increasing mist.

* * * * * * *

"Booshoh he!"—as, at the conclusion of an hour, some object at the extremity of the rope became indistinctly visible—"Booshoh he!" was the exclamation which burst from the lips of Ben-Levi.

"Booshoh he!—for shame!—it is a ram from the thickets of Engedi, and as rugged as the valley of Jehoshaphat!"

"It is a firstling of the flock," said Abel-Phittim, "I know him by the bleating of his lips, and the innocent folding of his limbs. His eyes are more beautiful than the jewels of the Pectoral, and his flesh is like the honey of Hebron."

"It is a fatted calf from the pastures of Bashan," said the Pharisee, "the heathen have dealt wonderfully with us!—let us raise up our voices in a psalm!—let us give thanks on the shawm and on the psaltery—on the harp and on the huggab—on the cythern and on the sackbut!"

It was not until the basket had arrived within a few feet of the Gizbarim, that a low grunt be-

VII. 10

trayed to their perception a *hog* of no common size.

"Now El Emanu!" slowly, and with upturned eyes ejaculated the trio, as, letting go their hold, the emaciated porker tumbled headlong among the Philistines, "El Emanu!—God be with us— *it is the unutterable flesh!*"

HOP-FROG

[Published in the *Flag of our Union*, 1849.]

I NEVER knew any one so keenly alive to a joke as the king was. He seemed to live only for joking. To tell a good story of the joke kind, and to tell it well, was the surest road to his favor. Thus it happened that his seven ministers were all noted for their accomplishments as jokers. They all took after the king, too, in being large, corpulent, oily men, as well as inimitable jokers. Whether people grow fat by joking, or whether there is something in fat itself which predisposes to a joke, I have never been quite able to determine; but certain it is that a lean joker is a *rara avis in terris*.

About the refinements, or, as he called them, the "ghost" of wit, the king troubled himself very little. He had an especial admiration for *breadth* in a jest, and would often put up with *length*, for the sake of it. Over-niceties wearied him. He would have preferred Rabelais' "Gargantua" to the "Zadig" of Voltaire: and, upon the whole, practical jokes suited his taste far better than verbal ones.

At the date of my narrative, professing jesters had not altogether gone out of fashion at court. Several of the great continental "powers" still retained their "fools," who wore motley, with caps and bells, and who were expected to be always ready with sharp witticisms, at a moment's notice, in consideration of the crumbs that fell from the royal table.

Our king, as a matter of course, retained his "fool." The fact is, he *required* something in the way of folly—if only to counterbalance the heavy wisdom of the seven wise men who were his ministers—not to mention himself.

His fool, or professional jester, was not *only* a fool, however. His value was trebled in the eyes of the king, by the fact of his being also a dwarf and a cripple. Dwarfs were as common at court, in those days, as fools; and many monarchs would have found it difficult to get through their days (days are rather longer at court than elsewhere) without both a jester to laugh *with,* and a dwarf to laugh *at.* But, as I have already observed, your jesters, in ninety-nine cases out of a hundred, are fat, round and unwieldy—so that it was no small source of self-gratulation with our king that, in Hop-Frog (this was the fool's name), he possessed a triplicate treasure in one person.

I believe the name "Hop-Frog" was *not* that given to the dwarf by his sponsors at baptism, but it was conferred upon him, by general consent of the seven ministers, on account of his inability to walk as other men do. In fact, Hop-

Frog could only get along by a sort of interjectional gait—something between a leap and a wiggle,—a movement that afforded illimitable amusement, and of course consolation, to the king, for (notwithstanding the protuberance of his stomach and a constitutional swelling of the head) the king, by his whole court, was accounted a capital figure.

But although Hop-Frog, through the distortion of his legs, could move only with great pain and difficulty along a road or floor, the prodigious muscular power which nature seemed to have bestowed upon his arms, by way of compensation for deficiency in the lower limbs, enabled him to perform many feats of wonderful dexterity, where trees or ropes were in question, or any thing else to climb. At such exercises he certainly much more resembled a squirrel, or a small monkey, than a frog.

I am not able to say, with precision, from what country Hop-Frog originally came. It was from some barbarous region, however, that no person ever heard of—a vast distance from the court of our king. Hop-Frog, and a young girl very little less dwarfish than himself (although of exquisite proportions, and a marvelous dancer), had been forcibly carried off from their respective homes in adjoining provinces, and sent as presents to the king, by one of his ever-victorious generals.

Under these circumstances, it is not to be wondered at that a close intimacy arose between the two little captives. Indeed, they soon became sworn friends. Hop-Frog, who, although he made a great deal of sport, was by no means popular, had it not in his power to render Trippetta many services; but *she*, on account of her grace and exquisite beauty (although a dwarf), was universally admired and petted; so she possessed much influence; and never failed to use it, whenever she could, for the benefit of Hop-Frog.

On some grand state occasion—I forgot what —the king determined to have a masquerade, and whenever a masquerade or anything of that kind, occurred at our court, then the talents both of Hop-Frog and Trippetta were sure to be called into play. Hop-Frog, in especial, was so inventive in the way of getting up pageants, suggesting novel characters, and arranging costumes, for masked balls, that nothing could be done, it seems, without his assistance.

The night appointed for the *fête* had arrived. A gorgeous hall had been fitted up, under Trippetta's eye, with every kind of device which could possibly give *éclat* to a masquerade. The whole court was in a fever of expectation. As for costumes and characters, it might well be supposed that everybody had come to a decision on such points. Many had made up their minds (as to what *rôles* they should assume) a week, or even a month, in advance; and, in fact, there was not a particle of indecision anywhere—except in the case of the king and his seven ministers. Why *they* hesitated I never could tell, unless they did it by way of a joke. More probably, they found it difficult, on account of being so fat, to make up their minds. At all events, time flew; and, as a last resort, they sent for Trippetta and Hop-Frog.

When the two little friends obeyed the summons of the king, they found him sitting at his wine with the seven members of his cabinet council; but the monarch appeared to be in a very ill humor. He knew that Hop-Frog was not fond of wine; for it excited the poor cripple almost to madness; and madness is no comfortable feeling. But the king loved his practical jokes, and took pleasure in forcing Hop-Frog to drink and (as the king called it) "to be merry."

"Come here, Hop-Frog," said he, as the jester and his friend entered the room; "swallow this bumper to the health of your absent friends, [here Hop-Frog sighed,] and then let us have the benefit of your invention. We want characters—*characters,* man,—something novel—out of the way. We are wearied with this everlasting sameness. Come, drink! the wine will brighten your wits."

Hop-Frog endeavored, as usual, to get up a jest in reply to these advances from the king; but the effort was too much. It happened to be the poor dwarf's birthday, and the command to drink his "absent friends" forced the tears to his eyes. Many large, bitter drops fell into the goblet as he took it, humbly from the hand of the tyrant.

"Ah! ha! ha! ha!" roared the latter, as the dwarf reluctantly drained the beaker. "See what a glass of good wine can do! Why, your eyes are shining already!"

Poor fellow! his large eyes *gleamed*, rather than shone; for the effect of wine on his excitable brain was not more powerful than instantaneous. He placed the goblet nervously on the table, and looked round upon the company with a half-insane stare. They all seemed highly amused at the success of the king's *"joke."*

"And now to business," said the prime minister, a *very* fat man.

"Yes," said the king; "Come, Hop-Frog, lend us your assistance. Characters, my fine fellow; we stand in need of characters—all of us—ha! ha! ha!" and as this was seriously meant for a joke, his laugh was chorused by the seven.

Hop-Frog also laughed although feebly and somewhat vacantly.

"Come, come," said the king, impatiently, "have you nothing to suggest?"

"I am endeavoring to think of something *novel*," replied the dwarf, abstractedly, for he was quite bewildered by the wine.

"Endeavoring!" cried the tyrant, fiercely; "what do you mean by *that?* Ah, I perceive. You are sulky, and want more wine. Here, drink this!" and he poured out another goblet full and offered it to the cripple, who merely gazed at it, gasping for breath.

"Drink, I say!" shouted the monster, "or by the fiends——"

The dwarf hesitated. The king grew purple with rage. The courtiers smirked. Trippetta pale as a corpse, advanced to the monarch's seat, and, falling on her knees before him, implored him to spare her friend.

The tyrant regarded her, for some moments, in evident wonder at her audacity. He seemed quite at a loss what to do or say—how most becomingly to express his indignation. At last, without uttering a syllable, he pushed her violently from him, and threw the contents of the brimming goblet in her face.

The poor girl got up the best she could, and, not daring even to sigh, resumed her position at the foot of the table.

There was a dead silence for about half a minute, during which the falling of a leaf, or of a feather, might have been heard. It was interrupted by a low, but harsh and protracted *grating* sound which seemed to come at once from every corner of the room.

"What—what—*what* are you making that noise for?" demanded the king, turning furiously to the dwarf.

The latter seemed to have recovered, in great measure, from his intoxication, and looking fixedly but quietly into the tyrant's face, merely ejaculated:

"I—I? How could it have been me?"

"The sound appeared to come from without," observed one of the courtiers. "I fancy it was the parrot at the window, whetting his bill upon his cage-wires."

"True," replied the monarch, as if much relieved by the suggestion; "but, on the honor of a knight, I could have sworn that it was the gritting of this vagabond's teeth.''

Hereupon the dwarf laughed (the king was too confirmed a joker to object to any one's laughing), and displayed a set of large, powerful, and very repulsive teeth. Moreover, he avowed his perfect willingness to swallow as much wine as desired. The monarch was pacified; and having drained another bumper with no very perceptible ill effect, Hop-Frog entered at once, and with spirit, into the plans for the masquerade.

''I cannot tell what was the association of idea,'' observed he, very tranquilly, and as if he had never tasted wine in his life, '' but *just* after your majesty had struck the girl and thrown the wine in her face—*just after* your majesty had done this, and while the parrot was making that odd noise outside the window, there came into my mind a capital diversion—one of my own country frolics—often enacted among us, at our masquerades: but here it will be new altogether. Unfortunately, however, it requires a company of eight persons and——''

''Here we *are!*'' cried the king, laughing at his acute discovery of the coincidence; ''eight to a fraction—I and my seven ministers. Come! what is the diversion?''

''We call it,'' replied the cripple, ''the Eight Chained Ourang-Outangs, and it really is excellent sport if well enacted.''

''*We* will enact it,'' remarked the king, drawing himself up, and lowering his eyelids.

"The beauty of the game," continued Hop-Frog, "lies in the fright it occasions among the women."

"Capital!" roared in chorus the monarch and his ministry.

"I will equip you as ourang-outangs," proceeded the dwarf; "leave all that to me. The resemblance shall be so striking, that the company of masqueraders will take you for real beasts—and of course, they will be as much terrified as astonished."

"Oh, this is exquisite!" exclaimed the king. "Hop-Frog! I will make a man of you."

"The chains are for the purpose of increasing the confusion by their jangling. You are supposed to have escaped, *en masse*, from your keepers. Your majesty cannot conceive the *effect* produced, at a masquerade, by eight chained ourang-outangs, imagined to be real ones by most of the company; and rushing in with savage cries, among the crowd of delicately and gorgeously habited men and women. The *contrast* is inimitable."

"It *must* be," said the king: and the council arose hurriedly (as it was growing late), to put in execution the scheme of Hop-Frog.

His mode of equipping the party as ourang-outangs was very simple, but effective enough for his purposes. The animals in question had, at the epoch of my story, very rarely been seen in any part of the civilized world; and as the imitations made by the dwarf were sufficiently beast-like and more than sufficiently hideous, their truthfulness to nature was thus thought to be secured.

The king and his ministers were first encased in tight-fitting stockinet shirts and drawers. They were then saturated with tar. At this stage of the process, some one of the party suggested feathers; but the suggestion was at once overruled by the dwarf, who soon convinced the eight, by ocular demonstration, that the hair of such a brute as the ourang-outang was much more efficiently represented by *flax*. A thick coating of the latter was accordingly plastered upon the coating of tar. A long chain was now procured. First, it was passed about the waist of the king, *and tied;* then about another of the party and also tied; then about all successively, in the same manner. When this chaining arrangement was complete, and the party stood as far apart from each other as possible, they formed a circle; and to make all things appear natural, Hop-Frog passed the residue of the chain in two diameters, at right angles, across the circle, after the fashion adopted, at the present day, by those who capture chimpanzees, or other large apes in Borneo.

The grand saloon in which the masquerade was to take place, was a circular room, very lofty, and receiving the light of the sun only through a single window at top. At night (the season for which the apartment was especially designed) it was illuminated principally by a large chandelier, depending by a chain from the centre of the skylight, and lowered, or elevated, by means of a

counter-balance as usual; but (in order not to
look unsightly) this latter passed outside the
cupola and over the roof.

The arrangements of the room had been left
to Trippetta's superintendence; but, in some par-
ticulars, it seems, she had been guided by the
calmer judgment of her friend the dwarf. At
his suggestion it was that, on this occasion, the
chandelier was removed. Its waxen drippings
(which, in weather so warm, it was quite impossible to prevent) would have been seriously detri-
mental to the rich dresses of the guests, who, on
account of the crowded state of the saloon, could
not *all* be expected to keep from out its centre
—that is to say, from under the chandelier. Additional sconces were set in various parts of the
hall, out of the way; and a flambeau, emitting
sweet odor, was placed in the right hand of each
of the Caryatides that stood against the wall—
some fifty or sixty altogether.

The eight ourang-outangs, taking Hop-Frog's
advice, waited patiently until midnight (when
the room was thoroughly filled with masqueraders) before making their appearance. No sooner
had the clock ceased striking, however, than they
rushed, or rather rolled in, all together—for the
impediments of their chains caused most of the
party to fall, and all to stumble as they entered.

The excitement among the masqueraders was
prodigious, and filled the heart of the king with
glee. As had been anticipated, there were not
a few of the guests who supposed the ferocious-
looking creatures to be beasts of *some* kind in

reality, if not precisely ourang-outangs. Many of the women swooned with affright; and had not the king taken the precaution to exclude all weapons from the saloon, his party might soon have expiated their frolic in their blood. As it was, a general rush was made for the doors; but the king had ordered them to be locked immediately upon his entrance; and, at the dwarf's suggestion, the keys had been deposited with *him*.

While the tumult was at its height, and each masquerader attentive only to his own safety (for, in fact, there was much *real* danger from the pressure of the excited crowd), the chain by which the chandelier ordinarily hung, and which had been drawn up on its removal, might have been seen very gradually to descend, until its hooked extremity came within three feet of the floor.

Soon after this, the king and his seven friends having reeled about the hall in all directions, found themselves, at length, in its centre, and, of course, in immediate contact with the chain. While they were thus situated, the dwarf, who had followed noiselessly at their heels, inciting them to keep up the commotion, took hold of their own chain at the intersection of the two portions which crossed the circle diametrically and at right angles. Here, with the rapidity of thought, he inserted the hook from which the chandelier had been wont to depend; and, in an instant, by some unseen agency, the chandelier-chain was drawn so far upward as to take the hook out of reach, and, as an inevitable consequence, to drag the ourang-outangs together in close connection, and face to face.

The masqueraders, by this time, had recovered, in some measure, from their alarm; and, beginning to regard the whole matter as a well-contrived pleasantry, set up a loud shout of laughter at the predicament of the apes.

"Leave them to *me!*" now screamed Hop-Frog, his shrill voice making itself easily heard through all the din. "Leave them to *me*. I fancy *I* know them. If I can only get a good look at them, *I* can soon tell who they are."

Here, scrambling over the heads of the crowd, he managed to get to the wall; when, seizing a flambeau from one of the Caryatides, he returned, as he went, to the centre of the room—leaped, with the agility of a monkey, upon the king's head—and thence clambered a few feet up the chain—holding down the torch to examine the group of ourang-outangs, and still screaming: "*I* shall soon find out who they are!"

And now, while the whole assembly (the apes included) were convulsed with laughter, the jester suddenly uttered a shrill whistle; when the chain flew violently up for about thirty feet—dragging with it the dismayed and struggling ourang-outangs, and leaving them suspended in mid-air between the sky-light and the floor. Hop-Frog, clinging to the chain as it rose, still maintained his relative position in respect to the eight maskers, and still (as if nothing were the matter) continued to thrust his torch down toward them, as though endeavoring to discover who they were.

So thoroughly astonished was the whole company at this ascent, that a dead silence, of about a minute's duration, ensued. It was broken by just such a low, harsh, *grating* sound, as had before attracted the attention of the king and his councillors when the former threw the wine in the face of Trippetta. But, on the present occasion, there could be no question as to *whence* the sound issued. It came from the fang-like teeth of the dwarf, who ground them and gnashed them as he foamed at the mouth, and glared, with an expression of maniacal rage, into the upturned countenances of the king and his seven companions.

"Ah, ha!" said at length the infuriated jester. "Ah, ha! I begin to see who these people *are* now!" Here, pretending to scrutinize the king more closely, he held the flambeau to the flaxen coat which enveloped him, and which instantly burst into a sheet of vivid flame. In less than half a minute the whole eight ourang-outangs were blazing fiercely, amid the shrieks of the multitude who gazed at them from below, horror-stricken, and without the power to render them the slightest assistance.

At length the flames, suddenly increasing in virulence, forced the jester to climb higher up the chain, to be out of their reach; and, as he made this movement, the crowd again sank, for a brief instant, into silence. The dwarf seized his opportunity, and once more spoke:

"I now see *distinctly*," he said, "what manner of people these maskers are. They are a great king and his seven privy-councillors,—a king who does not scruple to strike a defenceless girl, and his seven councillors who abet him in the outrage. As for myself, I am simply Hop-Frog, the jester—and *this is my last jest*."

Owing to the high combustibility of both the flax and the tar to which it adhered, the dwarf had scarcely made an end of his brief speech before the work of vengeance was complete. The eight corpses swung in their chains, a fetid, blackened, hideous, and indistinguishable mass. The cripple hurled his torch at them, clambered leisurely to the ceiling, and disappeared through the sky-light.

It is supposed that Trippetta, stationed on the roof of the saloon, had been the accomplice of her friend in his fiery revenge, and that, together, they effected their escape to their own country; for neither was seen again.

VII. 11

BON-BON

[Published in the *Southern Literary Messenger*, August, 1835.]

> Quand un bon vin meuble mon estomac
> Je suis plus savant que Balzac—
> Plus sage que Pibrac ;
> Mon bras seul faisant l'attaque
> De la nation Cossaque,
> La mettroit au sac ;
> De Charon je passerois le lac
> En dormant dans son bac ;
> J'irois au fier Eac,
> Sans que mon cœur fît tic ni tac,
> Présenter du tabac.
>
> —*French Vaudeville.*

THAT Pierre Bon-Bon was a *restaurateur* of uncommon qualifications, no man who during the reign of ——, frequented the little café in the cul-de-sac Le Febvre at Rouen, will, I imagine, feel himself at liberty to dispute. That Pierre Bon-Bon was, in an equal degree, skilled in the philosophy of that period is, I presume, still more especially undeniable. His *pâtés à la foie* were beyond doubt immaculate ; but what pen can do justice to his essays *sur la Nature*—his thoughts *sur l'Ame*—his observations *sur l'Esprit?* If his *omelettes*—if his *fricandeaux* were inestimable, what *littérateur* of that day

162

would not have given twice as much for an *"Idée de Bon-Bon"* as for all the trash of all the *"Idées"* of all the rest of the *savants?* Bon-Bon had ransacked libraries which no other man had ransacked—had read more than any other would have entertained a notion of reading—had understood more than any other would have conceived the possibility of understanding; and although, while he flourished, there were not wanting some authors at Rouen to assert "that his *dicta* evinced neither the purity of the Academy, nor the depth of the Lyceum"—although, mark me, his doctrines were by no means very generally comprehended, still it did not follow that they were difficult of comprehension. It was, I think, on account of their self-evidency that many persons were led to consider them abstruse. It is to Bon-Bon—but let this go no further— it is to Bon-Bon that Kant himself is mainly indebted for his metaphysics. The former was indeed not a Platonist, nor strictly speaking an Aristotelian—nor did he, like the modern Leibnitz, waste those precious hours which might be employed in the invention of a *fricassée* or, *facili gradú,* the analysis of a sensation, in frivolous attempts at reconciling the obstinate oils and waters of ethical discussion. Not at all. Bon-Bon was Ionic—Bon-Bon was equally Italic. He reasoned *a priori*—He reasoned *a posteriori*. His ideas were innate—or otherwise. He believed in George of Trebizond—He believed in Bossarion. Bon-Bon was emphatically a—Bon-Bonist.

I have spoken of the philosopher in his capac-

ity of *restaurateur*. I would not, however, have
any friend of mine imagine that, in fulfilling his
hereditary duties in that line, our hero wanted
a proper estimation of their dignity and importance. Far from it. It was impossible to say in
which branch of his profession he took the greater pride. In his opinion the powers of the intellect held intimate connection with the capabilities of the stomach. I am not sure, indeed, that
he greatly disagreed with the Chinese, who hold
that the soul lies in the abdomen. The Greeks at
all events were right, he thought, who employed
the same word for the mind and the diaphragm.*
By this I do not mean to insinuate a charge of
gluttony, or indeed any other serious charge to
the prejudice of the metaphysician. If Pierre
Bon-Bon had his failings—and what great man
has not a thousand?—if Pierre Bon-Bon, I say,
had his failings, they were failings of very little
importance—faults indeed which, in other tem-
pers, have often been looked upon rather in the
light of virtues. As regards one of these foibles,
I should not even have mentioned it in this history but for the remarkable prominency—the extreme *alto relievo*—in which it jutted out from
the plane of his general disposition. He could
never let slip an opportunity of making a
bargain.

Not that he was avaricious—no. It was by
no means necessary to the satisfaction of the
philosopher, that the bargain should be to his

* Φρένες.

own proper advantage. Provided a trade could be effected—a trade of any kind, upon any terms, or under any circumstances—a triumphant smile was seen for many days thereafter to enlighten his countenance, and a knowing wink of the eye to give evidence of his sagacity.

At any epoch it would not be very wonderful if a humor so peculiar as the one I have just mentioned, should elicit attention and remark. At the epoch of our narrative, had this peculiarity *not* attracted observation, there would have been room for wonder indeed. It was soon reported that, upon all occasions of the kind, the smile of Bon-Bon was found to differ widely from the downright grin with which he would laugh at his own jokes, or welcome an acquaintance. Hints were thrown out of an exciting nature; stories were told of perilous bargains made in a hurry and repented of at leisure; and instances were adduced of unaccountable capacities, vague longings, and unnatural inclinations implanted by the author of all evil for wise purposes of his own.

The philosopher had other witnesses—but they are scarcely worthy our serious examination. For example, there are few men of extraordinary profundity, who are found wanting in an inclination for the bottle. Whether this inclination be an exciting cause, or rather a valid proof of such profundity, it is a nice thing to say. Bon-Bon, as far as I can learn, did not think the subject adapted to minute investigation;—nor do I. Yet in the indulgence of a propensity so truly classical, it is not to be supposed that the *restaurateur* would lose sight of that intuitive discrimination which was wont to characterize, at one and the same time, his *essais* and his *omelettes*. In his seclusions the Vin de Bourgogne had its allotted hour, and there were appropriate moments for the Côtes du Rhone. With him Sauterne was to Medoc what Catullus was to Homer. He would sport with a syllogism in sipping St. Peray, but unravel an argument over Clos de Vougéot, and upset a theory in a torrent of Chambertin. Well had it been if the same quick sense of propriety had attended him in the peddling propensity to which I have formerly alluded—but this was by no means the case. Indeed to say the truth, *that* trait of mind in the philosophic Bon-Bon *did* begin at length to assume a character of strange intensity and mysticism, and appeared deeply tinctured with the *diablerie* of his favorite German studies.

To enter the little *café* in the *cul-de-sac* Le Febvre was, at the period of our tale, to enter the *sanctum* of a man of genius. Bon-Bon was a man of genius. There was not a *sous-cuisinier* in Rouen, who could not have told you that Bon-Bon was a man of genius. His very cat knew it, and forebore to whisk her tail in the presence of the man of genius. His large water-dog was acquainted with the fact, and upon the approach of his master, betrayed his sense of inferiority by a sanctity of deportment, a debasement of the ears, and a dropping of the lower jaw not altogether unworthy of a dog. It is, however, true that much of this habitual respect might have been attributed to the personal appearance of the metaphysician. A distinguished exterior will, I am constrained to say, have its way even with a beast; and I am willing to allow much in the outward man of the *restaurateur* calculated to impress the imagination of the quadruped. There is a peculiar majesty about the atmosphere of the little great—if I may be permitted so equivocal an expression—which mere physical bulk alone will be found at all times inefficient in creating. If, however, Bon-Bon was barely three feet in height, and if his head was diminutively small, still it was impossible to behold the rotundity of his stomach without a sense of magnificence nearly bordering upon the sublime. In its size both dogs and men must have seen a type of his acquirements—in its immensity a fitting habitation for his immortal soul.

I might here—if it so pleased me—dilate upon the matter of habiliment, and other mere circumstances of the external metaphysician. I might hint that the hair of our hero was worn short, combed smoothly over his forehead, and surmounted by a conical-shaped white flannel cap and tassels—that his pea-green jerkin was not after the fashion of those worn by the common class of *restaurateurs* at that day—that the sleeves were something fuller than the reigning costume permitted—that the cuffs were turned up, not as usual in that barbarous period, with cloth of the same quality and color as the garment, but faced in a more fanciful manner with the particolored velvet of Genoa—that his slippers were of a bright purple, curiously filigreed, and might have been manufactured in Japan, but for the exquisite pointing·of the toes, and the brilliant tints of the binding and embroidery—that his breeches were of the yellow satin-like material called *aimable*—that his sky-blue cloak, resembling in form a dressing-wrapper, and richly bestudded all over with crimson devices, floated cavalierly upon his shoulders like a mist of the morning—and that his *tout ensemble* gave rise to the remarkable words of Benevenuta, the Improvisatrice of Florence, "that is was difficult to say whether Pierre Bon-Bon was indeed a bird of Paradise, or the rather a very Paradise of perfection." I might, I say, expiate upon all these points if I pleased, —but I forbear; merely personal details may be left to historical novelists,—they are beneath the moral dignity of matter-of-fact.

I have said that "to enter the *café* in the *cul-de-sac* Le Febvre was to enter the *sanctum* of a man of genius"—but then it was only the man of genius who could duly estimate the merits of the *sanctum*. A sign, consisting of a vast folio, swung before the entrance. On one side of the volume was painted a bottle; on the reverse a *pâté*. On the back were visible in large letters *Œuvres de Bon-Bon*. Thus was delicately shadowed forth the twofold occupation of the proprietor.

Upon stepping over the threshold, the whole interior of the building presented itself to view.

A long, low-pitched room, of antique construction, was indeed all the accommodation afforded by the *café*. In a corner of the apartment stood the bed of the metaphysician. An array of curtains, together with a canopy *à la Grecque*, gave it an air at once classic and comfortable. In the corner diagonally opposite, appeared, in direct family communion, the properties of the kitchen and the *bibliothèque*. A dish of polemics stood peacefully upon the dresser. Here lay an ovenful of the latest ethics—there a kettle of duodecimo *mélanges*. Volumes of German morality were hand and glove with the gridiron—a toasting-fork might be discovered by the side of Eusebius—Plato reclined at his ease in the frying-pan—and contemporary manuscripts were filed away upon the spit.

In other respects the *Café de Bon-Bon* might be said to differ little from the usual *restaurants* of the period. A large fireplace yawned opposite the door. On the right of the fireplace an open cupboard displayed a formidable array of labelled bottles.

It was here, about twelve o'clock one night, during the severe winter of ——, that Pierre Bon-Bon, after having listened for some time to the comments of his neighbors upon his singular propensity—that Pierre Bon-Bon, I say, having turned them all out of his house, locked the door upon them with an oath, and betook himself in no very pacific mood to the comforts of a leather-bottomed arm-chair, and a fire of blazing fagots.

It was one of those terrific nights which are only met with once or twice during a century. It snowed fiercely, and the house tottered to its centre with the floods of wind that, rushing through the crannies of the wall, and pouring impetuously down the chimney, shook awfully the curtains of the philosopher's bed, and disorganized the economy of his pâté-pans and papers. The huge folio sign that swung without, exposed to the fury of the tempest, creaked ominously, and gave out a moaning sound from its stanchions of solid oak.

It was in no placid temper, I say, that the metaphysician drew up his chair to its customary station by the hearth. Many circumstances of a perplexing nature had occurred during the day, to disturb the serenity of his meditations. In attempting *des œufs à la Princesse,* he had unfortunately perpetrated an *omelette à la Reine;* the discovery of a principle in ethics had been frustrated by the overturning of a stew; and last, not least, he had been thwarted in one of those admirable bargains which he at all times took such especial delight in bringing to a successful termination. But in the chafing of his mind at these unaccountable vicissitudes, there did not fail to be mingled some degree of that nervous anxiety which the fury of a boisterous night is so well calculated to produce. Whistling to his more immediate vicinity the large black water-dog we have spoken of before, and settling himself uneasily in his chair, he could not help casting a wary and unquiet eye toward those distant recesses of the apartment whose inexorable shadows not even the red firelight itself could more than partially succeed in overcoming. Having completed a scrutiny whose exact purpose was perhaps unintelligible to himself, he drew close to his seat a small table covered with books and papers, and soon became absorbed in the task of retouching a voluminous manuscript, intended for publication on the morrow.

He had been thus occupied for some minutes, "I am in no hurry, Monsieur Bon-Bon," suddenly whispered a whining voice in the apartment.

"The devil!" ejaculated our hero, starting to his feet, overturning the table at his side, and staring around him in astonishment.

"Very true," calmly replied the voice.

"Very true!—what is very true?—how came you here?" vociferated the metaphysician, as his eye fell upon something which lay stretched at full length upon the bed.

"I was saying," said the intruder, without attending to the interrogatives,—"I was saying that I am not at all pushed for time—that the business upon which I took the liberty of calling, is of no pressing importance—in short, that I can very well wait until you have finished your Exposition."

"My Exposition!—there now!—how do *you*

know?—how came *you* to understand that I was writing an Exposition—good God!''

''Hush!'' replied the figure, in a shrill undertone; and, arising quickly from the bed, he made a single step toward our hero, while an iron lamp that depended over-head swung convulsively back from his approach.

The philosopher's amazement did not prevent a narrow scrutiny of the stranger's dress and appearance. The outlines of his figure, exceedingly lean, but much above the common height, were rendered minutely distinct by means of a faded suit of black cloth which fitted tight to the skin, but was otherwise cut very much in the style of a century ago. These garments had evidently been intended for a much shorter person than their present owner. His ankles and wrists were left naked for several inches. In his shoes, however, a pair of very brilliant buckles gave the lie to the extreme poverty implied by the other portions of his dress. His head was bare, and entirely bald, with the exception of the hinder-part, from which depended a *queue* of considerable length. A pair of green spectacles, with side glasses, protected his eyes from the influence of the light, and at the same time prevented our hero from ascertaining either their color or their conformation. About the entire person there was no evidence of a shirt; but a white cravat, of filthy appearance, was tied with extreme precision around the throat, and the ends hanging down formally side by side gave (although I dare say unintentionally) the idea of an ecclesiastic. Indeed, many other points both in his appearance and demeanor might have very well sustained a conception of that nature. Over his left ear, he carried, after the fashion of a modern clerk, an instrument resembling the *stylus* of the ancients. In a breast-pocket of his coat appeared conspicuously a small black volume fastened with clasps of steel. This book, whether accidentally or not, was so turned outwardly from the person as to discover the words, *"Rituel Catholique"* in white letters upon the back. His entire physiognomy was interestingly saturnine—even cadaverously pale. The forehead was lofty, and deeply furrowed with the ridges of contemplation. The corners of the mouth were drawn down into an expression of the most submissive humility. There was also a clasping of the hands, as he stepped toward our hero—a deep sigh—and altogether a look of such utter sanctity as could not have failed to be unequivocally prepossessing. Every shadow of anger faded from the countenance of the metaphysician, as, having completed a satisfactory survey of his visitor's person, he shook him cordially by the hand, and conducted him to a seat.

There would however be a radical error in attributing this instantaneous transition of feeling in the philosopher, to any one of those causes which might naturally be supposed to have had an influence. Indeed, Pierre Bon-Bon, from what I have been able to understand

of his disposition, was of all men the least likely
to be imposed upon by any speciousness of exterior deportment. It was impossible that so
accurate an observer of men and things should
have failed to discover, upon the moment, the
real character of the personage who had thus
intruded upon his hospitality. To say no more,
the conformation of his visitor's feet was sufficiently remarkable—he maintained lightly
upon his head an inordinately tall hat—there
was a tremendous swelling about the hinder part
of his breeches—and the vibration of his coat
tail was a palpable fact. Judge, then, with
what feelings of satisfaction our hero found
himself thrown thus at once into the society of
a person for whom he had at all times entertained the most unqualified respect. He was,
however, too much of the diplomatist to let escape him any intimation of his suspicions in regard to the true state of affairs. It was not
his cue to appear at all conscious of the high
honor he thus unexpectedly enjoyed; but, by
leading his guest into conversation, to elicit
some important ethical ideas, which might, in
obtaining a place in his contemplated publication, enlighten the human race, and at the same
time immortalize himself—ideas which, I
should have added, his visitor's great age, and
well-known proficiency in the science of morals,
might very well have enabled him to afford.

Actuated by these enlightened views, our hero
bade the gentleman sit down, while he himself
took occasion to throw some faggots upon the fire,

and place upon the now re-established table some
bottles of *Mousseux*. Having quickly completed
these operations, he drew his chair *vis-à-vis* to
his companion's, and waited until the latter
should open the conversation. But plans even
the most skilfully matured are often thwarted in
the outset of their application—and the *restaurateur* found himself *nonplussed* by the very
first words of his visitor's speech.

"I see you know me, Bon-Bon," said he;
"ha! ha! ha!—he! he! he!—hi! hi! hi!—ho! ho!
ho!—hu! hu! hu!"—and the Devil, dropping at
once the sanctity of his demeanor, opened to its
fullest extent a mouth from ear to ear, so as to
display a set of jagged and fang-like teeth, and,
throwing back his head, laughed long, loudly,
wickedly, and uproariously, while the black dog,
crouching down upon his haunches, joined lust-
ily in the chorus, and the tabby cat, flying off at
a tangent, stood up on end, and shrieked in the
farthest corner of the apartment.

Not so the philosopher: he was too much a
man of the world either to laugh like the dog,
or by shrieks to betray the indecorous trepidation of the cat. It must be confessed, he felt a
little astonishment to see the white letters which
formed the words *"Rituel Catholique"* on the
book in his guest's pocket, momently changing
both their color and their import, and in a few
seconds, in place of the original title, the words
"Regître des Condamnés" blaze forth in characters of red. This startling circumstance, when
Bon-Bon replied to his visitor's remark, im-

parted to his manner an air of embarrassment which probably might not otherwise have been observed.

"Why, sir," said the philosopher, "why, sir, to speak sincerely—I believe you are—upon my word—the d——dest—that is to say, I think— I imagine—I *have* some faint—some *very* faint idea of the remarkable honor——"

"Oh!—ah!—yes!—very well!" interrupted his Majesty; "say no more—I see how it is." And hereupon, taking off his green spectacles, he wiped the glasses carefully with the sleeve of his coat, and deposited them in his pocket.

If Bon-Bon had been astonished at the incident of the book, his amazement was now much increased by the spectacle which here presented itself to view. In raising his eyes, with a strong feeling of curiosity to ascertain the color of his guest's, he found them by no means black, as he had anticipated—nor gray, as might have been imagined—nor yet hazel nor blue—nor indeed yellow nor red—nor purple—nor white—nor green—nor any other color in the heavens above, or in the earth beneath, or in the waters under the earth. In short, Pierre Bon-Bon not only saw plainly that his Majesty had no eyes whatsoever, but could discover no indications of their having existed at any previous period—for the space where eyes should naturally have been was, I am constrained to say, simply a dead level of flesh.

It was not in the nature of the metaphysician to forbear making some inquiry into the sources

of so strange a phenomenon, and the reply of
his Majesty was at once prompt, dignified, and
satisfactory.

"Eyes! my dear Bon-Bon—eyes! did you say?
—oh!—ah!—I perceive! The ridiculous prints,
eh, which are in circulation, have given you a
false idea of my personal appearance? Eyes!—
true. Eyes, Pierre Bon-Bon, are very well in
their proper place—*that*, you would say, is the
head?—right—the head of a worm. To *you*,
likewise, these optics are indispensable—yet I
will convince you that my vision is more pene-
trating than your own. There is a cat I see in
the corner—a pretty cat—look at her—observe
her well. Now, Bon-Bon, do you behold the
thoughts—the thoughts, I say—the ideas—the
reflections—which are being engendered in her
pericranium? There it is, now—you do not!
She is thinking we admire the length of her tail
and the profundity of her mind. She has just
concluded that I am the most distinguished of
ecclesiastics, and that you are the most super-
ficial of metaphysicians. Thus you see I am not
altogether blind; but to one of my profession,
the eyes you speak of would be merely an in-
cumbrance, liable at any time to be put out by a
toasting-iron or a pitchfork. To you, I allow,
these optical affairs are indispensable. Endeavor, Bon-Bon, to use them well;—*my* vision
is the soul."

Hereupon the guest helped himself to the wine
upon the table, and pouring out a bumper for
    VII. 12

Bon-Bon, requested him to drink it without scruple, and make himself perfectly at home.

"A clever book that of yours, Pierre," resumed his Majesty, tapping our friend knowingly upon the shoulder, as the latter put down his glass after a thorough compliance with his visitor's injunction. "A clever book that of yours, upon my honor. It's a work after my own heart. Your arrangement of the matter, I think, however, might be improved, and many of your notions remind me of Aristotle. That philosopher was one of my most intimate acquaintances. I liked him as much for his terrible ill temper, as for his happy knack at making a blunder. There is only one solid truth in all that he has written, and for that I gave him the hint out of pure compassion for his absurdity. I suppose, Pierre Bon-Bon, you very well know to what divine moral truth I am alluding?"

"Cannot say that I——"

"Indeed!—why it was I who told Aristotle that by sneezing, men expelled superfluous ideas through the proboscis."

"Which is—hiccup!—undoubtedly the case," said the metaphysician, while he poured out for himself another bumper of Mousseux, and offered his snuff-box to the fingers of his visitor.

"There was Plato, too," continued his Majesty, modestly declining the snuff-box and the compliment it implied—"there was Plato, too, for whom I, at one time, felt all the affection of a friend. You knew Plato, Bon-Bon?—ah, no, I beg a thousand pardons. He met me at Athens,

one day, in the Parthenon, and told me he was
distressed for an idea. I bade him write down
that ὁ νοῦς ἔστιν αὐλός. He said that he would
do so, and went home, while I stepped over to
the pyramids. But my conscience smote me for
having uttered a truth, even to aid a friend, and
hastening back to Athens, I arrived behind the
philosopher's chair as he was inditing the 'αὐλός.'

"Giving the lambda a fillip with my finger, I
turned it upside down. So the sentence now
reads 'ὁ νοῦς ἔστιν αὐγός,' and is, you perceive,
the fundamental doctrines in his metaphysics."

"Were you ever at Rome?" asked the *restaurateur*, as he finished his second bottle of Mousseux, and drew from the closet a large supply of
Chambertin.

"But once, Monsieur Bon-Bon, but once.
There was a time," said the Devil, as if reciting
some passage from a book "there was a time
when occurred an anarchy of five years, during
which the republic, bereft of all its officers, had
no magistracy besides the tribunes of the people,
and these were not legally vested with any degree
of executive power—at that time, Monsieur Bon-
Bon—at that time *only* I was in Rome, and I
have no earthly acquaintance, consequently, with
any of its philosophy."*

"What do you think of—what do you think of
—hiccup—Epicurus?"

"What do I think of *whom?*" said the Devil,
in astonishment, "you surely do not mean to find

* Ils écrivaient sur la Philosophie (*Cicero, Lucretius, Sen-
eca*) mais c'était la Philosophie Grecque.—*Condorcet.*

any fault with Epicurus! What do I think of Epicurus! Do you mean me, sir?—I am Epicurus! I am the same philosopher who wrote each of the three hundred treatises commemorated by Diogenes Laertes.''

''That's a lie!'' said the metaphysician, for the wine had gotten a little into his head.

''Very well!—very well, sir!—very well, indeed, sir!'' said his Majesty, apparently much flattered.

''That's a lie!'' repeated the *restaurateur,* dogmatically; ''that's a—hiccup!—a lie!''

''Well, well, have it your own way!'' said the Devil, pacifically, and Bon-Bon, having beaten his Majesty at an argument, thought it his duty to conclude a second bottle of Chambertin.

''As I was saying,'' resumed the visitor—''as I was observing a little while ago, there are some very *outré* notions in that book of yours, Monsieur Bon-Bon. What, for instance, do you mean by all that humbug about the soul. Pray, sir, what *is* the soul?''

''The—hiccup!—soul,'' replied the metaphysician, referring to his MS., ''is undoubtedly——''

''No, sir!''

''Indubitably——''

''No, sir!''

''Indisputably——''

''No, sir!''

''Evidently——''

''No, sir!''

''Incontrovertibly——''

"No, sir!"

"Hiccup!——"

"No, sir!"

" And beyond all question, a——"

"No, sir, the soul is no such thing!" (Here the philosopher, looking daggers, took occasion to make an end, upon the spot, of his third bottle of Chambertin.)

"Then—hiccup!—pray, sir—what—what is it?"

"That is neither here nor there, Monsieur Bon-Bon," replied his Majesty, musingly. "I have tasted—that is to say, I have known some very bad souls, and some too—pretty good ones." Here he smacked his lips, and, having unconsciously let fall his hand upon the volume in his pocket, was seized with a violent fit of sneezing.

He continued.

"There was the soul of Cratinus—passable: Aristophanes—racy: Plato—exquisite—not *your* Plato, but Plato the comic poet; your Plato would have turned the stomach of Cerberus—faugh! Then let me see! there were Nævius, and Andronicus, and Plautus, and Terentius. Then there were Lucilius, and Catullus, and Naso, and Quintus Flaccus,—dear Quinty! as I called him when he sung a *seculare* for my amusement, while I toasted him, in pure good humor, on a fork. But they want *flavor*, these Romans. One fat Greek is worth a dozen of them, and besides will *keep*, which cannot be said of a Quirite. Let us taste your Sauterne."

Bon-Bon had by this time made up his mind to the *nil admirari,* and endeavored to hand down the bottle in question. He was, however, conscious of a strange sound in the room like the wagging of a tail. Of this, although extremely indecent in his Majesty, the philosopher took no notice:—simply kicking the dog, and requesting him to be quiet. The visitor continued:

"I found that Horace tasted very much like Aristotle;—you know I am fond of variety. Terentius I could not have told from Menander. Naso, to my astonishment, was Nicander in disguise. Virgilius had a strong twang of Theocritus. Martial put me much in mind of Archilochus—and Titus Livius was positively Polybius and none other."

"Hiccup!" here replied Bon-Bon, and his Majesty proceeded:

"But if I *have* a *penchant,* Monsieur Bon-Bon —if I *have* a *penchant,* it is for a philosopher. Yet, let me tell you, sir, it is not every dev—I mean it is not every gentleman who knows how to *choose* a philosopher. Long ones are *not* good; and the best, if not carefully shelled, are apt to be a little rancid on account of the gall."

"Shelled!"

"I mean taken out of the carcass."

"What do you think of a—hiccup!—physician?"

"*Don't* mention them!—ugh! ugh!" (Here his Majesty retched violently.) "I never tasted but one—that rascal Hippocrates!—smelt of asafœtida—ugh! ugh! ugh!—caught a wretched cold washing him in the Styx—and after all he gave me the cholera-morbus.''

''The—hiccup!—wretch!'' ejaculated Bon-Bon, ''the—hiccup!—abortion of a pill-box!''—and the philosopher dropped a tear.

''After all,'' continued the visitor, ''after all, if a dev—if a gentleman wishes to *live*, he must have more talents than one or two; and with us a fat face is an evidence of diplomacy.''

''How so?''

''Why we are sometimes exceedingly pushed for provisions. You must know that, in a climate so sultry as mine, it is frequently impossible to keep a spirit alive for more than two or three hours; and after death, unless picked immediately (and a picked spirit is *not* good), they will—smell—you understand, eh? Putrefaction is always to be apprehended when the souls are consigned to us in the usual way.''

''Hiccup!—hiccup!—good God; how *do* you manage?''

Here the iron lamp commenced swinging with redoubled violence, and the Devil half started from his seat;—however, with a slight sigh, he recovered his composure, merely saying to our hero in a low tone: ''I tell you what, Pierre Bon-Bon, we *must* have no more swearing.''

The host swallowed another bumper, by way of denoting thorough comprehension and acquiescence, and the visitor continued.

''Why, there are *several* ways of managing. The most of us starve: some put up with the pickle: for my part I purchase my spirits *vivente corpore,* in which case I find they keep very well.''

''But the body!—hiccup!—the body!!''

''The body, the body—well, what of the body? —oh! ah! I perceive. Why, sir, the body is not *at all* affected by the transaction. I have made innumerable purchases of the kind in my day, and the parties never experienced any inconvenience. There were Cain and Nimrod, and Nero, and Caligula, and Dionysius, and Pisistratus, and—and a thousand others, who never knew what it was to have a soul during the latter part of their lives; yet, sir, these men adorned society. Why isn't there A——, now, whom you know as well as I? Is *he* not in possession of all his faculties, mental and corporeal? Who writes a keener epigram? Who reasons more wittily? Who—but stay! I have his agreement in my pocket-book.''

Thus saying, he produced a red leather wallet, and took from it a number of papers. Upon some of these Bon-Bon caught a glimpse of the letters *Machi—Maza—Robesp*—with the words *Caligula, George, Elizabeth.* His Majesty selected a narrow slip of parchment, and from it read aloud the following words:

''In consideration of certain mental endowments which it is unnecessary to specify, and in further consideration of one thousand louis d'or, I, being aged one year and one month, do hereby make over to the bearer of this agreement all my right, title, and appurtenance in the shadow

called my soul. (Signed) A . . . ."*
(Here his Majesty repeated a name which I do
not feel myself justified in indicating more unequivocally.)

"A clever fellow that," resumed he; "but like
you, Monsieur Bon-Bon, he was mistaken about
the soul. The soul a shadow, truly! The soul
a shadow; Ha! ha! ha!—he! he! he!—hu! hu!
hu! Only think of a fricasséed shadow!"

"*Only* think—hiccup!—of a fricasséed shadow!" exclaimed our hero, whose faculties were
becoming much illuminated by the profundity
of his Majesty's discourse.

"Only think of a—hiccup!—fricasséed shadow!! Now, damme!—hiccup!—humph! If *I*
would have been such a—hiccup!—nincom-
poop! *My* soul, Mr.—humph!"

"*Your* soul, Monsieur Bon-Bon?"

"Yes, sir—hiccup!—*my* soul is——"

"What, sir?"

"*No* shadow, damme!"

"Did you mean to say——"

"Yes, sir, *my* soul is—hiccup!—humph!—yes,
sir."

"Did you not intend to assert——"

"*My* soul is—hiccup!—peculiarly qualified
for—hiccup!—a——"

"What, sir?"

"Stew."

"Ha!"

"Soufflée."

"Eh!"

* *Qnery.* — Arouet?

"Fricassée."

"Indeed!"

"Ragout and fricandeau—and see here, my good fellow; I'll let you have it—hiccup!—a bargain." Here the philosopher slapped his Majesty upon the back.

"Couldn't think of such a thing," said the latter calmly, at the same time rising from his seat. The metaphysician stared.

"Am supplied at present," said his Majesty.

"Hic-cup!—e-h?" said the philosopher.

"Have no funds on hand."

"What?"

"Besides, very unhandsome in me——"

"Sir!"

"To take advantage of——"

"Hic-cup!"

"Your present disgusting and ungentlemanly situation."

Here the visitor bowed and withdrew—in what manner could not precisely be ascertained—but in a well-concerted effort to discharge a bottle at "the villain," the slender chain was severed that depended from the ceiling, and the metaphysician prostrated by the downfall of the lamp.

THE DUC DE L'OMELETTE

[Published in the *Southern Literary Messenger*, February, 1836.]

And stepped at once into a cooler clime.—*Cowper.*

KEATS fell by a criticism. Who was it died of '' The Andromache?''* Ignoble souls!—De L'Omelette perished of an ortolan. *L'histoire en est brève.* Assist me, Spirit of Apicius!

A golden cage bore the little winged wanderer, enamored, melting, indolent, to the *Chaussée D'Antin,* from its home in far Peru. From its queenly possessor La Bellissima, to the Duc De L'Omelette, six peers of the empire conveyed the happy bird.

That night the Duc was to sup alone. In the privacy of his bureau he reclined languidly on that ottoman for which he sacrificed his loyalty in outbidding his king,—the notorious ottoman of Cadêt.

He buries his face in the pillow. The clock strikes! Unable to restrain his feelings, his Grace

---

* Montfleury. The author of the '' Parnasse Réformé'' makes him speak in Hades:—'' *L'homme donc qui voudrait savoir ce dont je suis mort, qu'il ne demande pas si'l fut de fièvre ou de podagre ou d'autre chose, mais qu'il entende que ce fut de ' L'Andromache.'* ''

swallows an olive. At this moment the door gently opens to the sound of soft music, and lo! the most delicate of birds is before the most enamored of men! But what inexpressible dismay now overshadows the countenance of the Duc?— "*Horreur! — chien! — Baptiste! — l'oiseau! ah, bon Dieu! cet oiseau modeste que tu as déshabillé de ses plumes, et que tu as servi sans papier!*" It is superfluous to say more:— the Duc expired in a paroxysm of disgust. * * *

"Ha! ha! ha!" said his Grace on the third day after his decease.

"He! he! he!" replied the Devil faintly, drawing himself up with an air of *hauteur.*

"Why, surely you are not serious," retorted De L'Omelette. "I have sinned—*c'est vrai*— but, my good sir, consider!—you have no actual intention of putting such—such—barbarous threats into execution."

"No *what?*" said his Majesty—"come, sir, strip!"

"Strip, indeed! very pretty i' faith! no, sir, I shall *not* strip. Who are you, pray, that I, Duc De L'Omelette, Prince de Foie-Gras, just come of age, author of the 'Mazurkiad,' and member of the Academy, should divest myself at your bidding of the sweetest pantaloons ever made by Bourdon, the daintiest *robe-de-chambre* ever put together by Rombêrt—to say nothing of the taking my hair out of paper—not to mention the trouble I should have in drawing off my gloves?"

"Who am I?—ah, true! I am Baal-Zebub,

Prince of the Fly. I took thee, just now, from a rose-wood coffin inlaid with ivory. Thou wast curiously scented, and labelled as per invoice. Belial sent thee,—my Inspector of Cemeteries. The pantaloons, which thou sayest were made by Bourdon, are an excellent pair of linen drawers, and thy *robe-de-chambre* is a shroud of no scanty dimensions.''

''Sir!'' replied the Duc, ''I am not to be insulted with impunity!—Sir! I shall take the earliest opportunity of avenging this insult!—Sir! you shall hear from me! In the meantime *au revoir!*''—and the Duc was bowing himself out of the Satanic presence, when he was interrupted and brought back by a gentleman in waiting. Hereupon his Grace rubbed his eyes, yawned, shrugged his shoulders, reflected. Having become satisfied of his identity, he took a bird's-eye view of his whereabouts.

The apartment was superb. Even De L'Omelette pronounced it *bien comme il faut.* It was not its length nor its breadth,—but its height— ah, that was appalling!—There was no ceiling— certainly none—but a dense whirling mass of fiery-colored clouds. His Grace's brain reeled as he glanced upward. From above, hung a chain of an unknown blood-red metal—its upper end lost, like the city of Boston, *parmi les nues.* From its nether extremity swung a large cresset. The Duc knew it to be a ruby; but from it there poured a light so intense, so still, so terrible, Persia never worshipped such—Gheber never imagined such—Mussulman never dreamed of

such when, drugged with opium, he has tottered
to a bed of poppies, his back to the flowers, and
his face to the God Apollo. The Duc muttered
a slight oath, decidedly approbatory.

The corners of the room were rounded into
niches. Three of these were filled with statues
of gigantic proportions. Their beauty was Gre-
cian, their deformity Egyptian, their *tout ensemble* French. In the fourth niche the statue was
veiled; it was *not* colossal. But then there was
a taper ankle, a sandalled foot. De L'Omelette
pressed his hand upon his heart, closed his eyes,
raised them, and caught his Satanic Majesty—
in a blush.

But the paintings!—Kupris! Astarte! As-
toreth!—a thousand and the same! And Rafaelle
has beheld them! Yes, Rafaelle has been here;
for did he not paint the ——? and was he not
consequently damned? The paintings!—the
paintings! O luxury! O love!—who, gazing on
those forbidden beauties, shall have eyes for the
dainty devices of the golden frames that besprinkled, like stars, the hyacinth and the porphyry
walls?

But the Duc's heart is fainting within him.
He is not, however, as you suppose, dizzy with
magnificence, nor drunk with the ecstatic breath
of those innumerable censers. *C'est vrai que de
toutes ces choses il a pensé beaucoup—mais!* The
Duc De L'Omelette is terror-stricken; for,
through the lurid vista which a single uncur-
tained window is affording, lo! gleams the most
ghastly of all fires!

Le pauvre Duc! He could not help imagining that the glorious, the voluptuous, the never-dying melodies which pervaded that hall, as they passed filtered and transmuted through the alchemy of the enchanted window-panes, were the wailings and the howlings of the hopeless and the damned! And there, too!—there!—upon the ottoman!— who could *he* be?—he, the *petitmaitre*—no, the Deity—who sat as if carved in marble, *et qui sourit*, with his pale countenance, *si amèrement?*

Mais il faut agir—that is to say, a Frenchman never faints outright. Besides, his Grace hated a scene—De L'Omelette is himself again. There were some foils upon a table—some points also. The Duc had studied under B——; *il avait tué ses six hommes.* Now, then, *il peut s' échapper.* He measures two points, and, with a grace inimitable, offers his Majesty the choice. *Horreur!* his Majesty does not fence!

Mais il joue!—how happy a thought!—but his Grace had always an excellent memory. He had dipped in the *"Diable"* of the Abbé Gualtier. Therein it is said *"que le Diable n'ose pas refuser un jeu d' écarté."*

But the chances—the chances! True—desperate; but scarcely more desperate than the Duc. Besides, was he not in the secret?—had he not skimmed over Père Le Brun?—was he not a member of the Club Vingt-un? *"Si je perds,"* said he, *"je serai deux fois perdu—*I shall be doubly damned—*voilà tout!* (Here his Grace shrugged his shoulders.) *Si je gagne, je revien-*

*drai à mes ortolans—que les cartes soient pré-
parées!''*

His Grace was all care, all attention—his Majesty all confidence. A spectator would have
thought of Francis and Charles. His Grace
thought of his game. His Majesty did not think;
he shuffled. The Duc cut.

The cards are dealt. The trump is turned—
it is—it is—the king! No—it was the queen.
His Majesty cursed her masculine habiliments.
De L'Omelette placed his hand upon his heart.

They play. The Duc counts. The hand is
out. His Majesty counts heavily, smiles, and
is taking wine. The Duc slips a card.

''C' est à vous à faire,'' said his Majesty, cutting. His Grace bowed, dealt, and arose from
the table *en presentant le Roi.*

His Majesty looked chagrined.

Had Alexander not been Alexander, he would
have been Diogenes; and the Duc assured his
antagonist in taking leave, *''que s'il n' eût pas
été De L'Omelette il n' aurait point d'objection
d'être le Diable.''*

THE ANGEL OF THE ODD

AN EXTRAVAGANZA

[Published in the *Columbian Magazine*, October, 1844.]

It was a chilly November afternoon. I had just consummated an unusually hearty dinner, of which the dyspeptic *truffe* formed not the least important item, and was sitting alone in the dining-room, with my feet upon the fender, and at my elbow a small table which I had rolled up to the fire, and upon which were some apologies for dessert, with some miscellaneous bottles of wine, spirit and *liqueur*. In the morning I had been reading Glover's "Leonidas," Wilkie's "Epigoniad," Lamartine's "Pilgrimage," Barlow's "Columbiad," Tuckermann's "Sicily," and Griswold's "Curiosities"; I am willing to confess, therefore, that I now felt a little stupid. I made effort to arouse myself by aid of frequent Lafitte, and, all failing, I betook myself to a stray newspaper in despair. Having carefully perused the column of "houses to let," and the column of "dogs lost," and then the two columns of "wives and apprentices runaway," I attacked

VII. 13

with great resolution the editorial matter, and,
reading it from beginning to end without understanding a syllable, conceived the possibility of
its being Chinese, and so re-read it from the end
to the beginning, but with no more satisfactory
result. I was about throwing away, in disgust,

> " This folio of four pages, happy work
> Which not even poets criticise,"

when I felt my attention somewhat aroused by
the paragraph which follows:

The avenues to death are numerous and strange. A
London paper mentions the decease of a person from a
singular cause. He was playing at "puff the dart,"
which is played with a long needle inserted in some
worsted, and blown at a target through a tin tube. He
placed the needle at the wrong end of the tube, and
drawing his breath strongly to puff the dart forward
with force, drew the needle into his throat. It entered
the lungs, and in a few days killed him.

Upon seeing this I fell into a great rage, without exactly knowing why. "This thing," I exclaimed, "is a contemptible falsehood—a poor
hoax—the lees of the invention of some pitiable
penny-a-liner—of some wretched concoctor of
accidents in Cocaigne. These fellows, knowing
the extravagant gullibility of the age, set their
wits to work in the imagination of improbable
possibilities—of odd accidents, as they term
them; but to a reflecting intellect " (like mine,
I added, in parentheses, putting my forefinger
unconsciously to the side of my nose,) "to a con-
templative understanding such as I myself pos-

sess, it seems evident at once that the marvellous increase of late in these 'odd accidents' is by far the oddest accident of all. For my own part, I intend to believe nothing henceforward that has any thing of the 'singular' about it.''

"Mein Gott, den, vat a vool you bees for dat!" replied one of the most remarkable voices I ever heard. At first I took it for a rumbling in my ears—such as a man sometimes experiences when getting very drunk—but, upon second thought, I considered the sound as more nearly resembling that which proceeds from an empty barrel beaten with a big stick; and, in fact, this I should have concluded it to be, but for the articulation of the syllables and words. I am by no means naturally nervous, and the very few glasses of Lafitte which I had sipped served to embolden me a little, so that I felt nothing of trepidation, but merely uplifted my eyes with a leisurely movement, and looked carefully around the room for the intruder. I could not, however, perceive any one at all.

"Humph!" resumed the voice, as I continued my survey, "you mus pe so dronk as de pig, den, for not zee me as I zit here at your zide."

Hereupon I bethought me of looking immediately before my nose, and there, sure enough, confronting me at the table sat a personage nondescript, although not altogether indescribable. His body was a wine pipe, or a rum-puncheon, or something of that character, and had a truly Falstaffian air. In its nether extremity were inserted two kegs, which seemed to answer all the purposes of legs. For arms there dangled from the upper portion of the carcass two tolerably long bottles, with the necks outward for hands. All the head that I saw the monster possessed of was one of those Hessian canteens which resemble a large snuff-box with a hole in the middle of the lid. This canteen (with a funnel on its top, like a cavalier cap slouched over the eyes) was set on edge upon the puncheon, with the hole toward myself; and through this hole, which seemed puckered up like the mouth of a very precise old maid, the creature was emitting certain rumbling and grumbling noises which he evidently intended for intelligible talk.

"I zay," said he, "you mos pe dronk as de pig, vor zit dare and not zee me zit ere; and I zay, doo, you most pe pigger vool as de goose, vor to dispelief vat iz print in de print. 'T iz de troof —dat it iz—eberry vord ob it."

"Who are you, pray?" said I, with much dignity, although somewhat puzzled; "how did you get here? and what is it you are talking about?"

"As vor ow I com'd ere," replied the figure, "dat iz none of your pizzness; and as vor vat I be talking apout, I be talk apout vat I tink proper; and as vor who I be, vy dat is de very ting I com'd here for to let you zee for yourzelf."

"You are a drunken vagabond," said I, "and I shall ring the bell and order my footman to kick you into the street."

"He! he! he!" said the fellow, "hu! hu! hu! dat you can't do."

"Can't do!" said I, "what do you mean?—I can't do what?"

"Ring de pell," he replied, attempting a grin with his little villainous mouth.

Upon this I made an effort to get up, in order to put my threat into execution; but the ruffian just reached across the table very deliberately, and hitting me a tap on the forehead with the neck of one of the long bottles, knocked me back into the arm-chair from which I had half arisen. I was utterly astounded; and, for a moment, was quite at a loss what to do. In the meantime, he continued his talk.

"You zee," said he, "it iz te bess vor zit still; and now you shall know who I pe. Look at me! zee! I am te *Angel ov te Odd*."

"And odd enough, too," I ventured to reply; "but I was always under the impression that an angel had wings."

"Te wing!" he cried, highly incensed, "vat I pe do mit te wing? Mein Gott! do you take me vor a shicken?"

"No—oh, no!" I replied, much alarmed, "you are no chicken—certainly not."

"Well, den, zit still and pehabe yourself, or I 'll rap you again mid me vist. It iz te shicken ab te wing, und te owl ab te wing, und te imp ab te wing, und te headteuffel ab te wing. Te angel ab *not* te wing, and I am te *Angel ov te Odd*."

"And your business with me at present is—is—"

"My pizzness!" ejaculated the thing, "vy vot

a low-bred puppy you mos pe vor to ask a gentleman und an angel apout his pizzness!''

This language was rather more than I could bear, even from an angel; so, plucking up courage, I seized a salt-cellar which lay within reach, and hurled it at the head of the intruder. Either he dodged, however, or my aim was inaccurate; for all I accomplished was the demolition of the crystal which protected the dial of the clock upon the mantel-piece. As for the Angel, he evinced his sense of my assault by giving me two or three hard consecutive raps upon the forehead as before. These reduced me at once to submission, and I am almost ashamed to confess that, either through pain or vexation, there came a few tears into my eyes.

''Mein Gott!'' said the Angel of the Odd, apparently much softened at my distress; ''mein Gott, te man is eder ferry dronk or ferry zorry. You mos not trink it so strong—you mos put de water in te wine. Here, trink dis, like a goot veller, und don't gry now—don't!''

Hereupon the Angel of the Odd replenished my goblet (which was about a third full of Port) with a colorless fluid that he poured from one of his hand bottles. I observed that these bottles had labels about their necks, and that these labels were inscribed ''Kirschenwasser.''

The considerate kindness of the Angel mollified me in no little measure; and, aided by the water with which he diluted my Port more than once, I at length regained sufficient temper to listen to his very extraordinary discourse. I cannot pretend to recount all that he told me, but I gleaned from what he said that he was the genius who presided over the *contretemps* of mankind, and whose business it was to bring about the *odd accidents* which are continually astonishing the skeptic. Once or twice, upon my venturing to express my total incredulity in respect to his pretensions, he grew very angry indeed, so that at length I considered it the wiser policy to say nothing at all, and let him have his own way. He talked on, therefore, at great length, while I merely leaned back in my chair with my eyes shut, and amused myself with munching raisins and flipping the stems about the room. But, by and by, the Angel suddenly construed this behavior of mine into contempt. He arose in a terrible passion, slouched his funnel down over his eyes, swore a vast oath, uttered a threat of some character which I did not precisely comprehend, and finally made me a low bow and departed, wishing me, in the language of the archbishop in "Gil-Blas," "*beaucoup de bonheur et un peu plus de bon sens.*"

His departure afforded me relief. The *very* few glasses of Lafitte that I had sipped had the effect of rendering me drowsy, and I felt inclined to take a nap of some fifteen or twenty minutes, as is my custom after dinner. At six I had an appointment of consequence, which it was quite indispensable that I should keep. The policy of insurance for my dwelling-house had expired the day before; and, some dispute having arisen, it was agreed that, at six, I should meet the board of directors of the company and settle the terms of a renewal. Glancing upward at the clock on the mantel-piece (for I felt too drowsy to take out my watch), I had the pleasure to find that I had still twenty-five minutes to spare. It was half-past five; I could easily walk to the insurance office in five minutes; and my usual siestas had never been known to exceed five and twenty. I felt sufficiently safe, therefore, and composed myself to my slumbers forthwith.

Having completed them to my satisfaction, I again looked toward the time-piece, and was half inclined to believe in the possibility of odd accidents when I found that, instead of my ordinary fifteen or twenty minutes, I had been dozing only three; for it still wanted seven and twenty of the appointed hour. I betook myself again to my nap, and at length a second time awoke, when, to my utter amazement, it *still* wanted twenty-seven minutes of six. I jumped up to examine the clock, and found that it had ceased running. My watch informed me that it was half-past seven; and, of course, having slept two hours, I was too late for my appointment. "It will make no difference," I said; "I can call at the office in the morning and apologize; in the meantime what can be the matter with the clock?" Upon examining it I discovered that one of the raisin-stems which I had been flipping about the room during the discourse of the Angel of the Odd had flown through the fractured crystal, and lodging, singularly enough, in the keyhole, with an end projecting outward, had thus arrested the revolution of the minute-hand.

"Ah!" said I; "I see how it is. This thing speaks for itself. A natural accident, such as *will* happen now and then!"

I gave the matter no further consideration, and at my usual hour retired to bed. Here, having placed a candle upon a reading-stand at the bed-head, and having made an attempt to peruse some pages of the "Omnipresence of the Deity," I unfortunately fell asleep in less than twenty seconds, leaving the light burning as it was.

My dreams were terrifically disturbed by visions of the Angel of the Odd. Methought he stood at the foot of the couch, drew aside the curtains, and, in the hollow, detestable tones of a rum-puncheon, menaced me with the bitterest vengeance for the contempt with which I had treated him. He concluded a long harangue by taking off his funnel cap, inserting the tube into my gullet, and thus deluging me with an ocean of Kirschenwasser, which he poured. in a continuous flood, from one of the long-necked bottles that stood him instead of an arm. My agony was at length insufferable, and I awoke just in time to perceive that a rat had run off with the lighted candle from the stand, but *not* in season to prevent his making his escape with it through the hole. Very soon, a strong suffocating odor assailed my nostrils; the house, I clearly perceived, was on fire. In a few minutes the blaze broke forth with violence, and in an incredibly brief period the entire building was wrapped in

flames. All egress from my chamber, except
through a window, was cut off. The crowd, however, quickly procured and raised a long ladder.
By means of this I was descending rapidly, and
in apparent safety, when a huge hog, about
whose rotund stomach, and indeed about whose
whole air and physiognomy, there was something
which reminded me of the Angel of the Odd,—
when this hog, I say, which hitherto had been
quietly slumbering in the mud, took it suddenly
into his head that his left shoulder needed
scratching, and could find no more convenient
rubbing-post than that afforded by the foot of
the ladder. In an instant I was precipitated,
and had the misfortune to fracture my arm.

This accident, with the loss of my insurance,
and with the more serious loss of my hair,—
the whole of which had been singed off by the
fire,—predisposed me to serious impressions, so
that, finally, I made up my mind to take a wife.
There was a rich widow disconsolate for the loss
of her seventh husband, and to her wounded
spirit I offered the balm of my vows. She
yielded a reluctant consent to my prayers. I
knelt at her feet in gratitude and adoration.
She blushed, and bowed her luxuriant tresses
into close contact with those supplied me, tem-
porarily, by Grandjean. I know not how the
entanglement took place, but so it was. I arose
with a shining pate, wigless; she in disdain and
wrath, half buried in alien hair. Thus ended
my hopes of the widow by an accident which
could not have been anticipated, to be sure, but

which the natural sequence of events had brought about.

Without despairing, however, I undertook the siege of a less implacable heart. The fates were again propitious for a brief period; but again a trivial incident interfered. Meeting my betrothed in an avenue thronged with the *élite* of the city, I was hastening to greet her with one of my best-considered bows, when a small particle of some foreign matter lodging in the corner of my eye, rendered me, for the moment, completely blind. Before I could recover my sight, the lady of my love had disappeared—irreparably affronted at what she chose to consider my premeditated rudeness in passing her by ungreeted. While I stood bewildered at the suddenness of this accident (which might have happened, nevertheless, to any one under the sun), and while I still continued incapable of sight, I was accosted by the Angel of the Odd, who proffered me his aid with a civility which I had no reason to expect. He examined my disordered eye with much gentleness and skill, informed me that I had a drop in it, and (whatever a "drop" was) took it out, and afforded me relief.

I now considered it high time to die, (since fortune had so determined to persecute me,) and accordingly made my way to the nearest river. Here, divesting myself of my clothes, (for there is no reason why we cannot die as we were born,) I threw myself headlong into the current; the sole witness of my fate being a solitary crow that had been seduced into the eating of brandy-saturated corn, and so had staggered away from his fellows.   No sooner had I entered the water than this bird took it into its head to fly away with the most indispensable portion of my apparel.   Postponing, therefore, for the present, my suicidal design, I just slipped my nether extremities into the sleeves of my coat, and betook myself to a pursuit of the felon with all the nimbleness which the case required, and its circumstances would admit.   But my evil destiny attended me still. As I ran at full speed, with my nose up in the atmosphere, and intent only upon the purloiner of my property, I suddenly perceived that my feet rested no longer upon *terra-firma;* the fact is, I had thrown myself over a precipice, and should inevitably have been dashed to pieces, but for my good fortune in grasping the end of a long guide-rope, which depended from a passing balloon.

As soon as I sufficiently recovered my senses to comprehend the terrific predicament in which I stood or rather hung, I exerted all the power of my lungs to make that predicament known to the æronaut overhead.   But for a long time I exerted myself in vain.   Either the fool could not, or the villain would not perceive me.   Meantime the machine rapidly soared, while my strength even more rapidly failed.   I was soon upon the point of resigning myself to my fate, and dropping quietly into the sea, when my spirits were suddenly revived by hearing a hollow voice from above, which seemed to be lazily humming an opera air. Looking up, I perceived the Angel of the Odd. He was leaning with his arms folded, over the rim of the car; and with a pipe in his mouth, at which he puffed leisurely, seemed to be upon excellent terms with himself and the universe. I was too much exhausted to speak, so I merely regarded him with an imploring air.

For several minutes, although he looked me full in the face, he said nothing. At length removing carefully his meerschaum from the right to the left corner of his mouth, he condescended to speak.

"Who pe you," he asked, "und what der teuffel you pe do dare?"

To this piece of impudence, cruelty, and affectation, I could reply only by ejaculating the monosyllable "Help!"

"Elp!" echoed the ruffian—"not I. Dare iz te pottle—elp yourself, und pe tam'd!"

With these words he let fall a heavy bottle of Kirschenwasser which, dropping precisely upon the crown of my head, caused me to imagine that my brains were entirely knocked out. Impressed with this idea, I was about to relinquish my hold and give up the ghost with a good grace, when I was arrested by the cry of the Angel, who bade me hold on.

"Old on!" he said; "don't pe in te urry—don't. Will you pe taken de odder pottle, or ave you pe got zober yet and come to your zenzes?"

I made haste, hereupon, to nod my head

twice—once in the negative, meaning thereby that I would prefer not taking the other bottle at present—and once in the affirmative, intending thus to imply that I *was* sober and *had* positively come to my senses. By these means I somewhat softened the Angel.

"Und you pelief, ten," he inquired, "at te last? You pelief, ten, in te possibility of te odd?"

I again nodded my head in assent.

"Und you ave pelief in *me,* te Angel of te Odd?"

I nodded again.

"Und you acknowledge tat you pe te blind dronk and te vool?"

I nodded once more.

"Put your right hand into your left hand preeches pocket, ten, in token ov your vull zubmission unto te Angel ov te Odd."

This thing, for very obvious reasons, I found it quite impossible to do. In the first place, my left arm had been broken in my fall from the ladder, and, therefore, had I let go my hold with the right hand, I must have let go altogether. In the second place, I could have no breeches until I came across the crow. I was therefore obliged, much to my regret, to shake my head in the negative—intending thus to give the Angel to understand that I found it inconvenient, just at that moment, to comply with his very reasonable demand! No sooner, however, had I ceased shaking my head than—

"Go to der teuffel, ten!" roared the Angel of the Odd.

In pronouncing these words, he drew a sharp knife across the guide-rope by which I was suspended, and as we then happened to be precisely over my own house, (which, during my peregrinations, had been handsomely rebuilt,) it so occurred that I tumbled headlong down the ample chimney and alit upon the dining-room hearth.

Upon coming to my senses, (for the fall had very thoroughly stunned me,) I found it about four o'clock in the morning. I lay outstretched where I had fallen from the balloon. My head grovelled in the ashes of an extinguished fire, while my feet reposed upon the wreck of a small table, overthrown, and amid the fragments of a miscellaneous dessert, intermingled with a newspaper, some broken glass and shattered bottles, and an empty jug of the Schiedam Kirschenwasser. Thus revenged himself the Angel of the Odd.

SILENCE—A FABLE

[Published in the *Baltimore Book*, 1839.]

" The mountain pinnacles slumber ; valleys, crags, and caves
are silent."—*Alcman.*

"LISTEN to *me*," said the Demon, as he placed
his hand upon my head. "The region of which
I speak is a dreary region in Libya, by the bor-
ders of the river Zäire, and there is no quiet
there, nor silence.

"The waters of the river have a saffron and
sickly hue; and they flow not onward to the
sea, but palpitate forever and forever beneath
the red eye of the sun with a tumultuous and
convulsive motion. For many miles on either
side of the river's oozy bed is a pale desert of
gigantic water-lilies. They sigh one unto the
other in that solitude, and stretch toward the
heavens their long and ghastly necks, and nod
to and fro their everlasting heads. And there
is an indistinct murmur which cometh out
from among them like the rushing of subterrene
water. And they sigh one unto the other.

"But there is a boundary to their realm—
the boundary of the dark, horrible, lofty forest.

There, like the waves about the Hebrides, the low underwood is agitated continually.   But there is no wind throughout the heaven.   And the tall primeval trees rock eternally hither and thither with a crashing and mighty sound.   And from their high summits, one by one, drop everlasting dews.   And at the roots strange poisonous flowers lie writhing in perturbed slumber. And overhead, with a rustling and loud noise, the gray clouds rush westwardly forever, until they roll, a cataract, over the fiery wall of the horizon.   But there is no wind throughout the heaven.   And by the shores of the river Zäire there is neither quiet nor silence.

"It was night, and the rain fell; and, falling, it was rain, but having fallen, it was blood. And I stood in the morass among the tall lilies, and the rain fell upon my head—and the lilies sighed one unto the other in the solemnity of their desolation.

"And, all at once, the moon arose through the thin ghastly mist, and was crimson in color. And mine eyes fell upon a huge gray rock which stood by the shore of the river, and was lighted by the light of the moon.   And the rock was gray, and ghastly, and tall,—and the rock was gray.   Upon its front were characters engraven in the stone; and I walked through the morass of water-lilies, until I came close unto the shore, that I might read the characters upon the stone.   But I could not decipher them. And I was going back into the morass, when the moon shone with a fuller red, and I turned and

VII. 14

looked again upon the rock, and upon the characters, and the characters were DESOLATION.

"And I looked upward, and there stood a man upon the summit of the rock; and I hid myself among the water-lilies that I might discover the actions of the man. And the man was tall and stately in form, and was wrapped up from his shoulders to his feet in the toga of old Rome. And the outlines of his figure were indistinct—but his features were the features of a deity; for the mantle of the night, and of the mist, and of the moon, and of the dew, had left uncovered the features of his face. And his brow was loftly with thought, and his eye wild with care; and, in the few furrows upon his cheek I read the fables of sorrow, and weariness, and disgust with mankind, and a longing after solitude.

"And the man sat upon the rock, and leaned his head upon his hand, and looked out upon the desolation. He looked down into the low unquiet shrubbery, and up into the tall primeval trees, and up higher at the rustling heaven, and into the crimson moon. And I lay close within shelter of the lilies, and observed the actions of the man. And the man trembled in the solitude;—but the night waned, and he sat upon the rock.

"And the man turned his attention from the heaven, and looked out upon the dreary river Zäire, and upon the yellow ghastly waters, and upon the pale legions of the water-lilies. And the man listened to the sighs of the water-lilies, and to the murmur that came up from among them. And I lay close within my covert and observed the actions of the man. And the man trembled in the solitude;—but the night waned and he sat upon the rock.

"Then I went down into the recesses of the morass and waded afar in among the wilderness of lilies, and called upon the hippopotami which dwelt among the fens in the recesses of the morass. And the hippopotami heard my call, and came, with the behemoth, unto the foot of the rock, and roared loudly and fearfully beneath the moon. And I lay close within my covert and observed the actions of the man. And the man trembled in the solitude;—but the night waned and he sat upon the rock.

"Then I cursed the elements with the curse of tumult; and a frightful tempest gathered in the heaven, where, before, there had been no wind. And the heaven became livid with the violence of the tempest—and the rain beat upon the head of the man—and the floods of the river came down —and the river was tormented into foam—and the water-lilies shrieked within their beds—and the forest crumbled before the wind—and the thunder rolled—and the lightning fell—and the rock rocked to its foundation. And I lay close within my covert and observed the actions of the man. And the man trembled in the solitude;—but the night waned and he sat upon the rock.

"Then I grew angry and cursed, with the curse of *silence,* the river, and the lilies, and the wind, and the forest, and the heaven, and the thunder, and the sighs of the water-lilies. And they became accursed, and *were still*. And the moon ceased to totter up its pathway to heaven—and the thunder died away—and the lightning did not flash—and the clouds hung motionless—and the waters sunk to their level and remained—and the trees ceased to rock—and the water-lilies sighed no more—and the murmur was heard no longer from among them, nor any shadow of sound throughout the vast illimitable desert. And I looked upon the characters of the rock, and they were changed; and the characters were SILENCE.

"And mine eyes fell upon the countenance of the man and his countenance was wan with terror. And, hurriedly, he raised his head from his hand, and stood forth upon the rock and listened. But there was no voice throughout the vast illimitable desert, and the characters upon the rock were SILENCE. And the man shuddered, and turned his face away, and fled afar off, in haste, so that I beheld him no more."

*   *   *   *   *   *   *

Now there are fine tales in the volumes of the Magi—in the iron-bound, melancholy volumes of the Magi. Therein, I say, are glorious histories of the Heaven, and of the Earth, and of the mighty sea—and of the Genii that overruled the sea, and the earth, and the lofty heaven. There were much lore too in the sayings which were said by the Sibyls; and holy, holy things were heard of old by the dim leaves that trembled around Dodona—but, as Allah liveth, that fable which the Demon told me as he sat by my side in the shadow of the tomb, I hold to be the most wonderful of all! And as the Demon made an end of his story, he fell back within the cavity of the tomb and laughed. And I could not laugh with the Demon, and he cursed me because I could not laugh. And the lynx which dwelleth forever in the tomb, came out therefrom, and lay down at the feet of the Demon, and looked at him steadily in the face.